Devil's Advocate

Devilish Desires Series, Book Eleven

THIS BOOK IS WRITTEN BY A HUMAN.

Published By Kissmet Publishing

CHAPTER ONE

Nick

I have it all, and it means absolutely nothing to me.

I could still feel the punch to the gut that was Zack's returning to claim Zoe, as I was about to seal the deal and make her mine. I could still smell the exact fragrance of the air when I stepped out onto the balcony, still hear my voice as I told her, "I can be whoever you want me to be, Zoe."

What the hell was I thinking? I wasted eight years of my life on one woman.

A woman not unlike B.J. McCaffrey, who was sitting across from me now, acting as opposing counsel. I glanced at her. As drop-dead gorgeous as she was, she was just another woman.

"Mr. Adams? Are we boring you?"

I could hear him somewhere on the edges of my thoughts, but it didn't matter to me.

Change myself. For a woman. Where was my pride? Where is my pride?

"Earth to Mr. Adams."

I turned my head slowly to face the judge.

He was a prick.

"Does the accused need another lawyer? Or are you going to continue to sit there and let him destroy himself on the stand?"

I stared at my client. He didn't even wear a tie.

"Yeah. I think I am." At first, I couldn't believe the words came out of my mouth. But they felt good. Felt right, somehow. "I'm sick of working my ass off on cases and having my clients ignore everything I tell them about their demeanor on the stand."

Judge Walters peered at my rival, B.J. McCaffrey. She shrugged. "Mr. Adams. Your job is to defend this man. Are you incapable of doing that?"

"I don't know."

Again, the judge and my opponent exchanged a look.

Pull it together, Nick. Find that damn pride of yours.

"Wait." My gaze ricochetted around the desk in front of me and finally fell on the yellow legal pad with my scribbled notes for the case. "I apologize, Your Honor. It's been a rough—"

Eight years? Two months? Life?

"—day. My apologies to the court."

"I repeat, your job is to defend this man. Are you capable of doing that?"

Damn. I just apologized. Can't you let it go?

I didn't have the time or patience for the existential crisis I was going through, but it would have none of it. It was bound to torture me all the same. Of course, the reason for it was undoubtedly her. The woman I loved—or thought I loved—was on her honeymoon with my best friend. And I was beginning to see how crazy it had been for me to wait around eight years for her. As a result, I was approaching thirty and still didn't know who I was. I straightened my back. This is what Zoe had brought me to.

"Yes, Your Honor. It won't happen again."

"It better not, Mr. Adams, or you won't see the inside of my courtroom again."

Yeah, yeah. You're in charge, big boy. We all get it.

"I'm going to do you a solid, Mr. Adams. It's late. I'm—"

He likes to use slang. He thinks it makes him look cool.

I managed to roll my eyes inwardly this time.

"—adjourn this court until one. I suggest you take the time to pull yourself together." He glanced at my client. The rail-thin, gray-haired, unshaven man sat with his mouth hanging open like a guppy. "You can get down now." The man nodded and Walters struck the desk with his gavel, glaring at me. "The court is adjourned."

I gathered my things, cursing quietly.

A hand with meticulously groomed nails pressed the sleeve of my suit. "Are you okay, Nick?" B.J. McCaffrey pushed a strand of her long, raven-colored hair behind her ear. Not only was she a stunner, she also had a sexy, not exactly gravelly, but...smoky, Demi Moore-ish voice.

I didn't even realize she was aware of my first name. She was gazing at me sympathetically, but it was a farce. Her law firm was intent on making mine appear foolish. Which, to be fair, was the same thing I was attempting to do to hers. That is, before I became stark raving mad and practically offered my law license to the judge.

"I'm fine," I said gruffly, riffling papers to avoid looking at her. "Like you care," I muttered under my breath, but it must have been loud enough for her to hear it.

"I do care. Can I...I don't know...help you somehow?"

It was the first time I'd ever seen her stumble with words.

I continued to sift through my notes. Her sympathy, instead of helping me, was making me come unraveled. "Yeah. You can stay the fuck away from me."

She withdrew her hand slowly. I instantly hated myself for saying it to her. I peered at her. Her eyes went from concerned to icy in degrees. She snatched her briefcase from her table and twisted to storm out. This time, it was me grabbing her arm.

"I'm sorry. I-I..."

She yanked free of my grasp and leaned in, spitting, "Save it." She finished her grand exit, charging through the short gate thing that separated us from the gallery and rushing out the door, taking her cute little, red-suit-wearing ass with her. I watched her leave, the gaunt, mousy-looking woman who she was representing trailing after her. At least the woman'd been smart enough to hire a shark to fight for her.

I ran a hand over my face. "Shit."

"What the hell is wrong with you?" my buffoon of a client raged behind me.

I spun, happy that he had given me another target for my self-loathing. "I told you not to disparage your ex-wife on the stand."

"Yeah. I didn't understand what that meant."

Oh, for fuck's sake.

I'd forgotten he was a moron.

I took a breath.

I'd forgotten he was an uneducated man.

But he couldn't have asked a question?

"It means talk bad about her."

"Talk bad about her? I didn't talk bad about her."

"You called her a 'no-account, deadbeat whore.'" That was approximately the time that I tuned out on his testimony.

"Well, yeah," he drawled. "She is one. That doesn't mean I was talking bad about her."

I clenched my fists. "Actually, it does. You need to refer to her nicely."

"Like call her a no-account, deadbeat slut?" he asked, honestly putting thought into the question. "I guess I can do that."

I sighed, surveying him. "You couldn't wear a tie, Alvis?"

He had, at least, worn a dress shirt and pants, rather than jeans.

I suppose I should be happy with that.

My client shifted his weight, looking off to the side for a moment before returning his gaze to mine. "I don't have one, okay?"

"Don't have—" I stopped myself. I pictured my walk-in closet. It was ginormous, and I'd added a built-in shoe rack, and an island sort of thing to hold the dozens and dozens of ties that I owned. I was a clothes whore.

He really doesn't own a tie?

The thought was so foreign to me it took several seconds for it to sink in.

Poor slob. I guess I should be showing him at least a modicum of patience.

"Why didn't you say something?" I asked in a gentler tone. "I would have been happy to get one for you."

He shrugged, again looking at me and then away.

"Listen," I clasped his shoulder, "I'm sorry for losing my shit earlier. It's...been a long week." *And the woman I love chose my best friend over me. Yeah, there's that.* "Why don't you let me make it up to you, and I'll buy you a sandwich."

He brightened. "Really? That would be great."

I stuffed my papers into my briefcase, and we headed out the swinging door my adversary had left through earlier. In the crowded atrium of the building was a cart similar to a wheelbarrow. Zoe would have deemed it "cute." I rolled my eyes at my observation. I couldn't stop thinking of the girl. A vendor sold food from it—although the wares came from a cooler to her right and the "wheelbarrow/cart" acted as a counter. Bags of chips were clipped to the poles rising to support the cart's striped canopy. It wouldn't have appeared very promising if I hadn't known that Meat Me in the Atrium served the best damned sandwiches in Denver. Perhaps in the whole state of Colorado. It always amazed me how people could make the same ingredients taste totally different from someone else's dish. I mean, Subway, Jimmy John's, all those chains use the same basic items—ham and bread, etcetera—but each had a unique flavor. Most people could probably distinguish between them in a blind taste test. We got in line behind the dozens of other customers who knew how good the place was, too.

"The line seems long, but it moves pretty quickly," I told my pro bono client, Alvis Mahafey. But when I turned to him, he had vanished. I searched the throng and spotted him with a young, blonde knockout.

What reason could she have to talk to him?

I recognized that the crowd had shuffled forward, and I hastened to keep in line then cast my gaze at the pair again. She had slipped an arm through his and was giggling about something. A faint noise sounded in my cranium, not even loud enough to be an alarm.

It's probably another lawyer who got him off on one of his many drunk and disorderlies or DUIs.

But something wasn't right. They were too close. The body language didn't look like lawyer/client. He wouldn't be stupid enough to get involved with someone and be seen publicly with them at the venue where his divorce proceedings were taking place, would he?

"Sir?"

I turned to face an annoyed salesclerk. "Uhh, yeah. Can I get one of those..." I took a step back to scan the nearby chalked menu, which was artfully written on a sandwich board. "...Legal Eagle Subs and..." I glanced toward the door, where I'd last seen my client. He was gone.

"Mustard, mayo, pickles, onion, lettuce, tomato?"

"Huh? Oh, yes. Everything but the tomato." Tomatoes were evil. "And I guess a...I don't know...turkey sandwich?"

She frowned. "Are you asking me or telling me?"

I shot her a scowl of my own. "Telling. And two Cokes."

"What do you want on the turkey?"

What would the imbecile want on his sandwich?

"Just give it to me plain."

She raised a brow.

"Please."

I finished my transaction, snatched my sandwiches—juggling them, my cans of Coke, and my briefcase—and scanned the atrium again. No Alvis in sight. Aware that many people ate on the stairs of the courthouse, I went outside. I found a spot at the base of a column where I could put my stuff down. Leaning against the stair wall, I unwrapped my sub while still hunting for my client. It was a beautiful, warm spring day, but it wasn't the sun making me sweat.

Where is he? Did he not hear the judge say to be back by one?

I checked my watch. Quarter to. When I lifted my gaze, I saw a flash of seductive red followed by a gray, shapeless blob. The Lady in Red and Alvis's wife marched up the steps. B.J. caught my eye and lowered her head. Eleanor Mahafey hesitated before passing me. "Where's Alvis?"

I wish I knew.

B.J. tugged on her elbow. "Come on. He's none of your business now." She avoided looking at me and dragged the woman away.

B.J. hadn't gone far, though, when she released a sigh and turned back. "You know it's almost one, don't you?"

"Yeah. I know," I grumbled.

She spun on her heel, and without another word, hurried into the courthouse.

I huffed. Of all the judges, Walters was not one to be late with. He was known for levying hefty fines. Taking one last look, I gathered everything and climbed the stairs. When Judge Walters made his grand entrance at one o'clock sharp, Alvis was nowhere to be seen. I was about to claim my client got hung up in traffic and ask for a continuance, when Alvis barged in the door.

"I'm here," he announced loudly. He loped toward me, lost his balance, and righted himself by placing his hand on a big, bald-headed man's shoulder.

"Excuse me, madam."

"Oh, no," I muttered under my breath.

When it seemed like he would go over the gate to the rail rather than through it, I reached for his arm, but he dodged, grinning at me and wagging his finger. "Uh-uh-uh." He hip checked the gate open but didn't go to his seat, instead, stumbling toward the bench.

"Alvis!" I hissed. "Come here! Alvis!"

But the fool continued on. I dove and caught him, wrestling him into his seat while he argued with me loudly.

"But I want to talk to the judge. Explain things to him."

"We'll get our chance," I tried to reassure him. "You need to quiet down. Shh."

"Mr. Adams?"

I glanced at the judge. "Yes, Your Honor."

He appeared to be a bit flabbergasted. Not that I could blame him. "Are you ready to proceed?"

"Uhh...Your Honor...I'd like to respectfully ask for a continuance. My client isn't...feeling well."

B.J. scrambled up, gesturing at Alvis. "Your honor. This man is clearly inebriated."

"Well, what say you, Mr. Mahafey? Are you inebriated?"

He shook his head loosely. "Nah." He looked around the room then leaned forward to "whisper" to the judge. "But I'm drunk as a skunk." He began to giggle like a hyena.

I jumped to my feet. Thoroughly disgusted with the man, I lost it. "Oh, for crying out loud!"

"Mr. Adams!" the judge warned.

"How the hell did you get this drunk so quickly?"

"Well, you were the one who's had me not drinking since we started this. It's no wonder the shots hit me so hard."

"Oh, so this is my fault."

"Mr. Adams!"

"Well, yeah. Sort'er." He scratched his head as if having an internal debate over just whose fault it was.

"This is ludicrous." I crammed my papers into my briefcase. I was so livid, I was shaking. "I'm done here. Done. Done. Done."

"Mr. Adams, control yourself or I'll find you in contempt of court," Walters blustered.

"Oh, great. You want to fine me?" I pulled out my wallet and threw hundreds on the table like I was tipping someone. "How much is it gonna be? 'Cause it will be totally worth it to tell this jackass exactly what I think of him."

"Jackass? Me?" Alvis sputtered.

The judge pounded his gavel. "Mr. Adams. You are hereby charged with contempt of court, and if you don't get control of yourself immediately, you'll discover what a night in jail will do to cool you off."

That got my attention. I ground my teeth together. "Yes, Your Honor."

Walters looked from me to B.J. "Counsel, approach the bench."

I released air through my teeth like a steam engine and marched up to the bench. Once there, I clutched my hips and turned as B.J. drew near more cautiously.

"Nick."

I blinked in surprise. I was shocked that the judge knew my first name.

"Listen. I know this job can be a bit...much. Believe me, I don't like watching failed marriages playing out in front of me day after day. But you have to maintain some semblance of proper behavior."

His being nice mitigated my anger. "Yes, Your Honor. I'm sorry."

"Perhaps you need a vacation, son." He glanced at my opponent. "I don't see any way we can continue this today. Speak to my clerk about getting on my docket again."

"Yes, Your Honor." B.J. said meekly.

"Now as for the contempt of court charge." He studied me.

"Yes, Your Honor. Do I pay the clerk or..."

"There will be no fine. You are hereby sentenced to twenty hours of community service."

"Community service?"

"Yes. Look it up, Mr. Adams."

Oh, I'm not Nick anymore.

"This case is dismissed without prejudice, and I will be retiring to my chambers for the rest of the day. These proceedings have given me a headache."

CHAPTER TWO

B.J.

I try to help a guy, and he jumps down my throat. Men were a perpetual disappointment to me. I don't know why I even let my concern show. It was a weakness, and I prided myself on not having those. Or at least not showing them. I found, as a woman, I had to present a professional façade to be taken seriously. Although, I swear that sometimes inside I still felt like a little grubby-faced girl choking on coal dust.

And of all the people to slip in front of. Nick Adams. As pretentious as he was hot. Was it that physical attraction I felt that made me crack, or the fact that I sensed a little boy in him to match my little girl? I entertained myself briefly with the thought of a young Nick, drowning in his father's suitcoat. I shook my head as my heels clicked along the crowded corridor of the courthouse.

He's the enemy.

What a stupid thing to do. Open myself up, leaving me vulnerable to the punch in the gut he gave me.

Fool.

I'd actually felt tears spring to my eyes for a moment. Well, no more. Nick Adams was part of the loathsome Adams, McGuire, and Drew firm my practice was currently trying to take down. He'd get no more sympathy from me.

I looked longingly at my place across from the courthouse, wanting nothing more than to escape into the silky sheets that I had on my bed at the moment. But I dutifully took a left and plodded toward the office. I was nothing if not dutiful. The glare from the gigantic gold letters that obnoxiously announced the presence of my firm, Zonderbond and Associates, burned my corneas. As I entered, the security guard nodded at me, doing a very poor job of acting like he wasn't checking out my legs. Old pervert.

The unexpectedly short day meant that I could work on some depositions and draft a settlement proposal. Although it was barely one, the office was unusually empty. But it was Friday. That meant something to someone who had a life. My boss, Greg Zonderbond, stuck his head into the hall.

"Hey, B.J., do you have a moment?"

We both knew it didn't matter to him if I did or not. "Sure." I checked around. A few people were still in the vicinity. I wasn't totally alone with him. He gave me the creeps. There'd been one incident when he "accidentally" brushed my chest. And another, when he was drunk at a Christmas party, and he ran his hand up my leg, telling me he had "big plans" for me. Ugh! He'd made me a junior partner to keep me from leaving, but everyone knew who was in charge at the firm, and it certainly wasn't me.

I purposely left the door open when I entered his office. He leaned casually against his desk.

"Well, come on over here."

My heart beat erratically, but I tried to make sure it didn't show on my face. I walked toward him.

"Come on. Have a seat." He indicated a rolling chair less than a foot from his shin.

I attempted to be subtle as I sat, scooting the chair back as far as could be done naturally.

He shifted so that his legs were close to mine. So close, I could feel the heat emanating from his skin. "We haven't talked in a while. How are things?"

"Oh, good. Good." I hated the way my voice shook. "I've been billing a lot of hours," I said more confidently.

"Oh, I'm sure you have," he said dismissively. "How is the Mahafey case going?"

He wanted to hear about my pro bono case? Strange... I cleared my throat. "The judge dismissed it today without prejudice. I'll have to file again as soon as possible."

He frowned. "Why did he dismiss it?"

"Alvis Mahafey was drunk when he returned from lunch break."

He smiled and lifted his gaze slightly. I twisted in my chair to try to catch what he was peering at. Our receptionist, Michelle, was holding up her nails and admiring them, having painted them on company time. It was common knowledge that the two were sleeping together. Michelle was an absolutely worthless receptionist. I was pretty confident she had some other skills that weren't readily apparent to anyone other than Greg and any of the men she had bedded in the past.

Greg grasped my chin and rotated it so that I was forced to face him straight on. "Focus, B.J. Focus." As he said the last, his attention wandered to my cleavage. I sat straighter and leaned away. He tilted his head, staring at me intensely, sending a shiver along my spine. It was that look I'd seen him use while cross-examining witnesses, making them come unraveled. He stood and turned his back to stroll behind his desk.

I began to breathe more freely.

"Nick Adams is representing the husband, isn't he?" The information he gathered and retained never failed to amaze me. A strip of polished wood, front and center on his desk, read "Knowledge is power." He could be subtle, but he always got his point across. He reminded me of a giant spider with his legs sticking in a myriad of pies. Not a spider, a centipede.

"Uhh, yes. Nick—"

"I understand that he recently went through a breakup with a woman he'd been seeing for several months. Talk has it he was even seen picking out a diamond ring for her."

This surprised me. Nick had impressed me as the playboy type who could never be in a serious relationship. "I wouldn't know anything about that."

He leaned forward, lacing his fingers on his desk. "Adams, McGuire, and Drew have stolen several clients from us of late."

From what I'd heard, it was more a case of us being unsuccessful in our attempts to steal their clients. Greg seemed to have an unusual preoccupation with besting Adams, McGuire, and Drew, especially Nick Adams.

"I need for you to do something for me, B.J."

"Okay," I responded tentatively.

He picked up a crystal paperweight and spun it in his hand. "Nick Adams is probably vulnerable right now." He set the paperweight down suddenly and rose, going to the door to close it. I rotated my chair so as not to have my back to him. "I need for you to seduce him."

Was he serious? "What?"

He grabbed the arms of my chair and jerked me toward him. "I'm not asking you to sleep with him, necessarily..." He touched a strand of my hair, and I went rigid. "Simply loosen up some. Ask him to dinner..."

"Wouldn't that be a huge conflict of interest?"

He rolled a shoulder. "It happens. What we don't want, B.J., is for *your* interests to conflict with ours. The firm's. We need you to be a team player."

I shoved my chair backward, wrenching it from his grasp, and stood. "I will not seduce a man to win a case," I said icily. "I will get the outcome we want by using my legal skills."

"You'd better," he said evenly.

I'd had enough of his crap. "What is that supposed to mean?"

"Nothing. But...things are pretty rough these days. We may have to scale down a little around here, to meet budget."

"Are you threatening to take my job away from me because I'm not agreeing to sleep with the opposing counsel?"

"Of course not. But...results do matter. And I employ only the best." He focused on his computer screen. "You're dismissed."

Just like that?

I slowly turned and headed for the door, then I twisted. "What do you care about a divorce case? A pro bono divorce case?"

"Oh, I don't. But Clint McGuire has a case that could win us millions. And if someone were to get access to some private information that could help us... Well, it would go a long way toward their continued employment." He looked up from his computer screen. "We'll talk later. You can leave now. And...ask Michelle to come in here, please."

I went to my office but couldn't concentrate. Right when I was getting ready to pack it in, Greg stopped by. He leaned against my door jamb. "Have you thought through what I asked?"

I don't know if being in my office emboldened me, or what it was, but I rose and circled my desk, sitting on its edge to purposely mimic his earlier position. I crossed my arms and stared at him silently for a moment. "I don't like being backed into a corner, Mr. Zonderbond, and when I am, I come out swinging. It's one of the reasons you hired me."

Little by little he shifted his weight away from the doorframe until he was upright. Continuing my boxing analogy, he said, "I guess you better hope that you're the heavyweight that you think you are then." He glared at me unnervingly and left.

I exhaled slowly, my posture deflating as I did. I lifted a trembling hand to my forehead, brushing my dark hair aside. I needed this job. I had a hefty mortgage to pay, and a lifestyle I needed to maintain.

But I'd be damned if I let someone force me to compromise my principles.

CHAPTER THREE

Nick

Since my day had been so stellar, I decided not to waste any time and trotted over to a bar called Unwarranted across from the courthouse. They catered to the many lawyers in the vicinity, using the slogan, "For all your pour behavior, we're so good we're criminal." I was trying to work my way through the list titled Misdemeanors on the cocktail menu, which was comprised mostly of beer choices. So far, I'd had the Curb Appeal Bail Ale, the Jury's Out Stout, and the Acquit Ale, which was an I.P.A., I think. But I hadn't reached an appropriate level of numbness, so I decided to go hard and choose from the drinks marked under Felonies, which were a bit more lethal. I enjoyed the Subpoena Colada and followed it with the Grand Blurry.

I created a mini tornado in my tumbler by swirling it around as I stared into the golden-brown liquid within.

Probably the color of the sand on the beach they're sitting on in Maui.

Although I wouldn't know. I'd never been there. I'd spent my time working my tail off to purchase cars, a luxury condo with expensive furniture, designer clothing...all to impress Zoe, who was making love now with Zack. That thought had me raising the glass and downing its contents. Then I held it up to get the bartender's attention.

He moseyed toward me, wiping his hands on a towel. "What next?"

"I was eyeing the Dispute ReSolution."

He nodded. "Good choice."

I watched him pour, imagining the alcohol stream as a Hawaiian waterfall.

Fuck. Why can't I get you out of my fucking mind, Zoe? You're gone, and my dwelling on it won't bring you back.

I was a fool, amassing wealth and possessions, while she was with a gym teacher who'd probably never worn any piece of clothing with a designer label attached to it. In fact, he'd probably never worn anything that wasn't off the rack at a discount department store. His only accessory was a whistle. He couldn't tell Carhart from Cartier.

Yet she's with him.

And, I'll admit, he'd looked sharp on their wedding day, even in a rented tux. They'd invited me, as we were trying to reestablish our friendship, but they said they'd understand if I didn't want to come. Of course, I saw that as a challenge and came to show them how over her I was. Although, clearly, I wasn't. The liquor went down with that same burning that I'd felt seeing Zoe in her wedding dress. She'd looked absolutely phenomenal, which, while taking my breath away, wasn't a shock. That beautiful woman had been mine.

I sneered. *That's one thing you can't change, Zackie-boy. I had her before you did.* I chuckled at first, but it slowed and came to a hollow end. *Yeah, but he has her forever.*

The only images that were more painful than the two of them together were the ones of the two of us together. When we were wrapped up in each other, rolling in her bed, going at it full steam. The time we'd done it on the balcony. Thrilling, even without someone watching. I remembered her face glowing in the moonlight. And when we were done, we collapsed into the lounger, and I held her, having stolen a throw blanket from the couch to cover ourselves with.

But it wasn't just the sex. It was that time when she was on the counter, scared shitless by a little mouse. Her excitement when I flew her to see *Hamilton* in New York. How she twirled her hair around her finger when she was anxious. The way she was with kids. The style she used when swinging her hips to distract me on the ball court. Her jumping on my back when we were walking home from the pub.

Ugh.

Then I was lost in the memories. They spilled like well-worn pictures onto the bar top, soft with age, torn in places, and frequently handled. For a more concrete image, I slipped a photo of her from my breast pocket. I took it that night in New York. She was sitting across from me at Lamasseria, the candlelight making her face more mesmerizing than ever. I stared at the candle on the bar, feeling a tad fuzzy. Without thinking, I dipped a corner of the picture into the flame and caught it on fire. It rolled up, the burning leisurely working inward to Zoe's beautiful face.

"Hey, Mack!" The burly new bartender snatched it from me and tapped its edges on the bar top, ashy flakes breaking off. "You can't do that. This shit is flammable." He scowled at me. The fire extinguished, he examined the picture and whistled long and low. He lifted his gaze finally. "She mean somethin' to you?"

"She did."

His eyes widened, and he nodded exaggeratedly, peering again at Zoe. He seemed at a loss for words until he murmured, "That's a shame, man. A real shame."

Tell me about it.

"Do you want me to...?" He moved his arm back and forth to indicate throwing it in the nearby trash can.

I thought. "No. Not yet."

He handed it to me almost reverently, taking one last look. "*Real* shame."

I checked out the damage.

Why the hell did I burn it up? I didn't want to burn it up. I just wanted it to stop hurting.

"Need another?" my sympathetic mixologist asked.

"Yeah." I glanced at the menu. "I'm torn between the Show Us The Proof and the May It Please The Quart."

"Why not have both?"

I slapped the bar, a little harder than I meant to. "Why not indeed? Good man."

As I slid the picture back into my pocket, I felt the cold, metal ring and withdrew it. The diamond's facets sparkled in the candlelight. It was supposed to be hers. It had a nearly five-carat, emerald-cut center stone set in platinum, with another tapered diamond on each side. She would have hated it. She wasn't into objects; she was into Zack. I allowed myself to fantasize about me being the man at the end of the aisle. Zoe gliding toward me.

"We would have been good together, Zo," I whispered.

It was getting late, and I needed to go, but I wasn't ready. Having finished my two "felonies," I ordered a third, Libel Libation. I was stalling, not wanting to return to an empty condo again. A vacant space where her laughter once rang out. I set the ring on a coaster.

I'm such a sap.

Part of me wanted to leave it there and walk away. The other part of me knew it cost an insane amount of money and picked it up. Someone tapped on my shoulder. I spun to face them. Once square with the speaker, I stopped, but my brain kept rotating a time or two. A man with a good three days' worth of stubble stood in front of me in a wrinkled suit.

"You're in my seat."

"I am?" I looked between my legs at the stool I was sitting on. "Huh. It doesn't have your name on it." I turned back to the bar.

He tapped me again.

My jaw tightened.

"Yeah. But it's still my seat."

I'd had it. I whirled around. "Listen, buddy," I said through clenched teeth, "I've been sitting here all night, and I'm going to continue to sit here until I decide to leave, so beat it."

"Hmm." He looked to the side then took a swing.

I brought my arm up and blocked it with surprising speed, considering all the "felonies" I had under my belt. "What the fuck?" I shoved him to give me room to stand. "You just made a *big* mistake."

CHAPTER FOUR

B.J.

It was late, and I was stepping off the elevator and into the lobby. Not having been able to sleep, I'd slipped on a sweatsuit and headed to the private gym on the main floor of my twenty-five-story condo building. The Randolph was like its own city, with shops, restaurants, a hair stylist, tailor... Pretty much the only places I ever went to were the courthouse, the office, and The Randolph. Oh, and the dentist. The Randolph didn't have any dentists.

When I had insomnia, I often came down to tire myself on the stationary bike. But tonight, a barrage of noises met me as I exited the elevator, and the sound had me pulling up short. It was coming from one of the bars/restaurants to the right of the front door.

"I'm telling you, that's my seat." A guy in a wrinkled and bloodied blue suit was being dragged out by a police officer. A gash was open on his forehead.

"And I'm telling you, no one owns the seats in there."

"What about that possession being nine-tenths of the law thing? I was...what do they call that? ...Squatting! I was squatting," he screamed triumphantly.

"Here's the thing though," the policeman retorted, "in order to squat, you have to squat somewhere. And everyone in there says the other guy was sitting there peacefully when you walked in and started a fight. So, if anything, he was the squatter."

He sighed. "Listen. I'm having a bad day."

The officer frowned. "I'm afraid it's about to get worse."

I didn't hear the guy's reply as the other party was being hauled into the lobby. The other party being Nick Adams. He was looking kind of rough.

"For the ninth time," the policeman was saying, "I'm taking you in for assault. I'm not calling you a cab."

"Good," Nick responded. "I prefer merlot anyway." He sniggered, and the cop joined in.

"You're a funny one."

Nick straightened, his expression proud. "Thanks."

"I'm still arresting you."

Nick shrugged. "At least you'll be amused while you do it."

"True."

Recognizing the officer dealing with him from one of my cases, I ran forward.

"Hey. Hey, Mike." I caught up with them.

"Oh, hey, B.J."

I gazed at Nick. His bottom lip was split, but he was grinning. "What's going on?"

Mike Crawford smiled at me. "Oh, nothing to worry about. Only a scuffle between two drunks." He started to turn, but I put my hand on his arm, which probably wasn't a good idea as he jerked away like I was going for his gun.

"Sorry," I said demurely. I glanced at Nick. "It's just...this is my friend."

The officer's brows rose. "He is?"

"Yes. And he's had a really bad day." I poured on the charm, giving Mike a grin. "He went up against me in court, and you know that's never good." I laughed, and he chuckled too.

"I take it he lost, then?"

Movement caught my eye, and I shifted my gaze, spotting Nick sticking his tongue out at me. Trying not to frown, I tore my focus from him, continuing my little act. "Well, of course, he did."

"Ahh."

"Nick, here isn't a troublemaker. I heard he was minding his own business when that other man came in."

"Yeah. That's what people said," he admitted.

"See, he's not a threat to anyone. Could you maybe do me a favor? Could you...release Nick? I'll take him to my place and make sure he doesn't get into any more trouble."

"I don't know. He did exchange blows with someone. That guy—," he gestured at the revolving door through which we could see his partner and his charge watching us, "—may want to press charges against Mr. Adams."

But I could tell Mike was thinking about it. "If he does, I promise to bring Nick down tomorrow to answer for them."

He hesitated.

"Come on," I wheedled. "It's late. You don't want to have to fill out the paperwork on this little altercation. You can hardly even call it a fight. More like a tiff."

"A tiff that almost required stitches."

I glanced at Nick. He pantomimed throwing a punch with his free arm, nearly causing him to fall off balance. Mike helped him to stay on his feet.

"I don't know, B.J." He eyeballed Nick. "He's really snockered. Are you sure you can handle him?"

I drew on my reputation as a badass, grasping my hips. "Sure I can handle him? Have we met? Of course, I can handle him."

Mike assessed me, looked at Nick again, then at me.

I pushed. "You're just taking him to your precinct house and releasing him in a little while on his own recognizance anyway. I'll be saving you a hassle."

He glanced at his partner—who stared at him askance—and held up a finger.

"Okay. I'll help you as far as the elevator, then you're on your own."

I squeezed my hands together in glee. “Great.” I hurried toward the elevator before he could change his mind. “That’s great, Mike. I really appreciate it.” I stabbed at the button, and as late as it was, no one had called for it, and it was still on the first floor. It opened, and I gripped Nick’s shoulders, escorting him into the elevator and turning.

Mike sighed. “Don’t make me regret this.”

“Oh, you won’t, Mike. I really owe you.” His eyes brightened with the last, in a way I didn’t appreciate, and I jabbed at my floor button. “Good night.”

Nick, taking that as a cue, waved at him, then leaned to look around Mike and waved at his opponent. I’m not a lip reader, but it was clear even to me that the guy glared at his arresting officer and said, “What the fuck?”

Nick snickered, and the doors closed. “Sucker.”

I frowned at him. “You’re a mess. You need to get your shit together, Nick.”

He hung his head momentarily.

“You’re your own worst enemy,” I muttered, staring at the lights over the door.

He ignored me. “You’re taking me to your place?” he asked suggestively, wriggling his brows. He grabbed my hips and pulled me into him. “For some sexy time?”

I had to laugh but disentangled myself from him. “I doubt you could manage any sexy time at the moment, even if I were so inclined, which I’m not,” I added.

“Oh, come on.” He pawed at me again. “I’m good in be-ed...” he added in a singsong voice.

I’ve no doubt about that.

“That may be, but the farthest you’re getting is the couch tonight.”

He pouted. “You’re no fun.”

I sighed, leaning against the rear rail. “So they tell me.” I continued to stare at the numbers.

I am fun. If someone would give me a chance. If I could let someone see me without them walking all over me.

He took my hand gently, and my gaze snapped to him. As drunk as he'd been moments before, he seemed stone-cold sober. "I'm sorry."

To my surprise, I found myself blinking back tears.

The door dinged open on my floor. "Where are we going?" he slurred.

So, he wasn't sober. I marched with him to my condo and opened the door. "Come on. You're sleeping it off on my couch."

His brow furrowed as if he was figuring out my statement. "Have I ever done that before?"

"Nope. Alexa, turn the lights on low." That command lit a tall floor lamp in one corner, and a lamp on a side table. I waved him in then followed, unzipping my jacket. "And you never will again. I only give people one shot. Don't blow it."

He whistled. "Wow! This is some place."

I looked around. "Thank you." I'd forgotten how nice it was and assessed it anew, feeling a sense of accomplishment. When I was distracted with that, he stepped forward, not realizing, I guess, that the living room was sunken. He went sprawling. "Oh, Nick." I rushed to him, chastising myself for not foreseeing that. "Are you hurt?"

I helped him to a sitting position, his limbs as loose as Raggedy Ann's. I held his shoulders, keeping him from collapsing to the floor again. He rubbed his lips. "I hurt my mouth."

I smirked. "You did that yourself earlier."

He plopped a hand on the top of my head heavily and clumsily felt my face, finding my lips. I was so surprised, I didn't move. "Your mouth isn't cut."

He was a very attractive man, and it had been quite some time since I'd let any man touch me. "That's because I didn't get into a boxing match with my fellow bar patron."

"Oh." His fingers slowed, and he traced my lips. My heart rate accelerated. "You have a sexy mouth."

I knew he was drunk, and it didn't mean anything, but I felt myself warming all the same. I needed to get some distance between us. I cleared my throat. "We need to get you to the couch. Do you think you can stand?"

As I was talking, he crawled on his hands and knees to the couch.

I shook my head, amused. "Or that will work, I suppose."

But instead of getting on the couch, he sat in front of it.

"I'm tired."

"No, no, no, Nick. Up on the couch. You need to get up on the couch."

By the time I'd gotten to him, he'd turned sideways, drawing his knees in partially and leaning on the front of the couch. I shifted behind him, slid my arms through his and tried to lift him, but he wasn't cooperating at all. "That doesn't look very comfortable. Why don't we try the couch?"

Why am I talking to him like he's a child?

Because he's acting like a child. I answered myself.

"No," he muttered. "Leave me alone. I want to sleep."

I fell back onto my tush, sweating and breathing hard. I was getting my workout after all.

Do I just let him sleep on the floor?

It didn't seem right. He'd be sore in the morning.

Then again, he'll have other pain to worry about in the morning.

As if reading my thoughts, he moaned. "Ooh. I don't feel so good. I think I drank too much."

"Really?" I rolled my eyes. "What were you drinking anyway?"

"The Felonies," he mumbled.

"Which one?" I'd visited the place myself and suddenly had an urge for a Subpoena Colada.

"All of them."

"*All* of them?" I hopped to my feet. "I'll get you a trash can."

He moaned again.

I increased my pace. "Don't you throw up on my floor, Nick Adams. I just had the carpets cleaned."

I entered the bathroom and snagged the trash can, hearing a faint, "I should throw up on the couch then?"

"No! Not on the couch." I rushed into the living room but stopped short. He had crawled onto the couch and was lying on his stomach, his arm hanging limply over the side, his knuckles dragging on the floor. His mouth was open, and he was snoring, loudly.

I inhaled.

Well, well, counselor. Not your best look.

But I had to smile. I set the trash can on the floor by his head and slipped his shoes off, placing them on the floor near the couch. I had some difficulty yanking my throw blanket from under him and was about to leave it and get something from the linen closet when he snorted, quit snoring, and shifted slightly. Enough that it came free. I waited to see if he would wake, but his rhythmic breathing began again, although it was quieter. I stretched the blanket across him and pulled it to his shoulders. I paused, crouched in front of him. His face seemed almost angelic in the lamplight. I knew it was a lie. This was Nick Adams. He'd slept with every female in our building and the one adjacent to it. Or was it just rumors? If it was, he'd done nothing to discourage it.

I reached to slowly sweep away a section of hair that had fallen in his face. Free to examine him up close, my gaze roamed over his face. "You'll feel like shit in the morning, friend," I said softly, sighing. I straightened and turned to leave, but he called out. I twisted back, but he was quiet. I found the ibuprofen and got a glass of water from the kitchen, setting them on the glass-topped coffee table near him. An article that I'd read earlier in the day concerning a boy at the University of Denver being hazed and choking to death on his vomit flashed through my brain. Then another, from a few months ago, about a 24-year-old rock star who did the same.

I can't leave him here by himself.

I got that extra blanket from the closet and curled up in the chair next to him, switching the lamp off. Even then, I couldn't close my eyes for fear of him choking, and me not hearing.

He called out several times, but the last time he said it clearly. Zoe.

So, he cares about some girl. Maybe he's not the ladies' man he's painted himself to be. Maybe he's not shallow at all. Maybe, like me, he hides behind a reputation, plays a role, to protect himself.

I wondered who Zoe was, what had happened to her, what she was like. At some point I must have fallen asleep.

CHAPTER FIVE

N*ick*

I woke with a start, and a rolling stomach. I was facedown and drooling. I groaned. I could hear somebody breathing nearby.

Did I bring someone to my place?

Groaning, I struggled my head up. A woman was sleeping in a chair that was pulled unnaturally close to the couch. I shut my eyes and laid back on the cushion.

Why is that woman sleeping in a chair? WHO is that woman?

I searched my memory, but I couldn't get past this fantasy I'd been having with B.J. McCaffrey and me in an elevator. I'd said something that hurt her...

Why am I dreaming about B.J. McCaffrey, besides the obvious reasons?

I attributed it to having seen her earlier in the day and the fact that I was insanely attracted to her. Then I remembered how rude I'd been to her after the case was dismissed and understood why my dream had turned out the way it had. I tried to stop dreaming and go to sleep because my head was throbbing.

Ironically, when I peeled my eyes open next, the first thing I saw was an ibuprofen bottle and glass of water sitting on a table in front of me. From a long bank of windows across from me the sun was blaring into the room like a radio at full volume, stabbing my corneas. My mouth was so dry, my tongue was sticking to my teeth, and my face hurt.

Why does my face hurt?

I dared to open my eyes but only a slit.

Why is that ibuprofen bottle way over there?

It wasn't really that far from me; it was within two feet. But reaching for it seemed like a monumental effort. I shut my eyes and slapped my hand on the table, fumbling around, searching for the painkillers and nearly upsetting the glass of water. As I reeled the plastic container in, even the sound of the pills crashing against its side was horrendous.

I have to sit so I can swallow these pills.

I pushed off the couch, wondering just where I was, as it clearly wasn't my place. I groaned with the effort.

Damn. My shoulder hurts. What the hell did I do to myself?

I sat still, waiting for my head to stop its revolutions. With the utmost care, I got the glass of water, but the burning piercing my shoulder caused me to pause, so I could shake it and perhaps work it out. Popping the cap from the bottle with my thumb, I watched it fly somewhere. I poured four pills into my palm, threw them into my mouth, and washed them down with the water. The liquid returning to my body made it sigh.

Whoever left these pills for me was a complete angel, and I should ask them to marry me, whether they're male or female.

I drank more and cast my gaze around the room, taking care not to move too much. White furniture, white carpeting, glass and wrought iron tables, nice lamps... I quickly shifted my focus back to the coffee table, realizing I'd seen a magazine there, and it might help me to figure out where I was. I narrowed my eyes to read the title. "Law Practice" from the American Bar Association. Could I be...? I flipped it, hunting for the address. Barbara Jean McCaffrey. So that was her name.

Well, I'll be damned. B.J. McCaffrey brought me to her place. I'm in B.J. McCaffrey's home.

Since I was fully dressed, it was clear she hadn't had her way with or ravaged me... Could she have helped me? The Ice Princess of Colfax Avenue?

Something caught my attention, and I was interested enough to unfold myself from the couch, like an antique accordion. Once upright, I crossed to the pillar thing I'd seen and circled it. What appeared to be...a welding helmet? ...sat atop it. I gingerly took it off to examine it. It was interesting, even sexy, with sharp lines that made it look more like a motorcycle helmet than something to prevent someone from getting burned. Hearing footsteps, then a piercing shriek, I turned. B.J. McCaffrey stood before me sporting flannel boxers and a ribbed tank, one hand over her heart, one attempting to cover her body.

"Nick. I didn't think you'd be up."

Clearly.

My curiosity piqued, I skipped preliminaries and burst out with, "What's this?"

"Uhh...that's my welding hood. I did some welding in law school."

"Hmm..." I strode over to her, trying to be smooth. "It's kind of sexy. You should wear it for me."

Everything changed in an instant. She no longer seemed to care that she was practically naked in front of me. Okay, practically naked was an exaggeration. Or maybe hopeful thinking. Whatever the case, it was more of her than I'd ever seen, and it was a good view. Before my eyes she transformed. She straightened slowly, a notch at a time, and her face hardened. She went from college-dorm-room B.J. to scary-courtroom B.J. within seconds.

She plucked the helmet from my hand, giving me a stern look, and returned it to its stand. She stared at it a moment as if frozen, not saying anything.

"I've kept it to remind me of who I am, where I came from, and how far I've gotten."

Okay. I don't get it, but I'll take your word on it.

She became reanimated, seeming more like her former, college coed self. "Excuse me. I'll just go and get changed into something more appropriate. I'll be back momentarily." She kept switching from her usual stoic self into a real human being. It was throwing me. Maybe being at home made her relax.

Then she disappeared, and I stood gaping. Trying to absorb all the information our interaction had given me.

This is to remind me of who I am? What? A welder?

I wanted to ask, badly, but the way she reacted gave me the impression I shouldn't, although I wasn't sure if I could respect her wishes and keep quiet on the subject for long.

Why would one enshrine a welding helmet?

I walked around the room, searching for more clues as to who B.J. McCaffrey was, as, clearly, there was more to her than a courtroom shark. My biggest clue was the fact that there were no clues. Besides the magazine, there were no more legal materials, no knickknacks, not a scrap of anything that could tell me something. The place was so pristine it was almost sterile. Then I spotted a second display pillar on the other side of the room, this one with a cowgirl hat on it. I threw a look over my shoulder, but all was quiet in the hall. I stole across to examine it. It was made with a white, velvety material and had no embellishments except for a simple, braided, white, leather cord.

So, in addition to being a welder, she was a ranch hand, too? This makes no sense. The girl has a room full of nothing personal except for a welding helmet and a cowgirl hat. What was I supposed to make of that?

I set the cowgirl hat down carefully, trying to put it in its original position so she wouldn't be able to tell I touched it, then returned to the helmet. I heard her heels clicking on the hardwood floors of the hall and hurried back to the couch. She entered before I could sit, though, but I acted like I had just gotten to my feet.

She glanced from the pedestal I'd rushed from to me as she spoke. Had she caught movement when she entered? She peered at me suspiciously for a second then thankfully leapt into an apology. She was dressed in a knockout, three-piece, gray suit with the coat open and nothing under the vest. I resisted the urge to fall to my knees in front of her and worship. "I'm sorry about that earlier. Like I said, I thought with the short night of sleep we had that you'd still be snoozing."

"It's me who should be apologizing to you, I think...my memory's a little fuzzy on the details. And thanking you from...keeping me from being arrested?" I said the last as a question because I wasn't sure if it was part of the dreams I had or a memory.

A huge smile slid across her face. "Yes, that did happen."

I could feel my face heat. "I may have had too much to drink." Normally I would have boasted over that. But, being with her, outside of a courthouse, made me feel...different. I don't know why.

"*All* of the felonies?"

I looked down, then raised my gaze, wincing slightly. "Is it wrong that I'm a tiny bit proud of that?"

"In so many ways. Can I make you some breakfast, counselor?"

I covered my stomach as it balked at the thought. "Oh, hell no." I grinned. "But thank you." I slid my shoes on, sneaking a peak at hers. I don't know how she balanced on that toothpick of a heel, but she had killer legs.

"What about just a piece of toast? Or peanut butter toast?"

Is she trying to get me to stay?

I wish.

As I walked to the door, she followed behind me. "Thank you for the offer, but I really don't think it would be wise to introduce one more item to my stomach." I turned with my hand on the doorknob.

"Oh." She definitely looked disappointed.

Is she lonely?

"I really appreciate you letting me crash on your couch...and convincing the cop not to lock me up...and for the ibuprofen and water..." I opened the door and grasped it, my palm flat against the back of it, fingers curled around the edge. She was close, and every inch of me was aware of that. Without giving it much thought, I leaned in and kissed her cheek. As I pulled away, my gaze flitted over her face. "I owe you," I said, my voice rough.

I didn't leave.

She searched my face, her lips parted, and we stood frozen like that. Then it was like someone pushed play. "Oh, no big deal," she said dismissively. "You would have done the same."

Would I have? To be honest, I'd probably only have done it if I knew something was in it for me. I wasn't like her, or at least the B.J. I'd come to see in the last several hours. I thought we were more alike, and I respected that side of her—the hard-ass, tough-as-nails attorney—but she appeared to have a heart after all.

Oddly, that drew me to her even more. The juxtaposition of the B.J. I thought I knew, and the one I'd discovered yesterday, was like a jumbled puzzle, and I yearned to put the pieces together.

CHAPTER SIX

B.J.

"Wow."

I spun slowly from the door.

He kissed me.

Oh, shut up, B.J. So, he kissed you. He probably kisses his Aunt Marge, too.

He was just thankful that I'd gotten him out of a mess. He would have done the same.

Would he though? Nick Adams? He probably would have laughed as they hauled me off to jail.

So, seeing him asleep woke something in me. Everybody looked like an angel when they slept. My dad's voice swept in.

He told you to stay the fuck away from him. Did you forget that?

My heart grew heavy and hard in seconds, like it was filled with quick-set concrete. I went about finishing my morning routine robotically, pushing all thought of Nick Adams aside. All the emotions he had stirred.

You're not nineteen anymore. You know what they're all after. You know that they will use you, IF YOU LET THEM.

I wouldn't let them. Er...him. Nick Adams. The player of players. He could destroy my heart with a flick of a finger. Now it was his voice that haunted me.

Stay the fuck away from me.

I slapped my comb down on the sink and stared at myself in the mirror.

I'll stay the fuck away from you alright. ...Why did I help him? He's such a prick. I should have just let Mike haul him to jail. A night there would have done him good.

I shook my head at myself then went about straightening my hair. Albeit a bit violently.

Once at work, I buried myself in case notes to remove that image of Nick sleeping on my couch. And it helped. Until a man approached the reception desk with a huge bouquet of flowers. I glanced up from my desk, catching him through the glass front of my office but didn't give it another thought and returned to my paperwork. A few minutes later, Michelle rapped on my door. She was holding the bouquet.

Probably coming to gloat.

I waved her in, and she entered. To discourage her from believing that she had found someone to revel in her little flower victory with her, I asked curtly, "What can I do for you?"

She held out the vase. "These are for...you." She looked hurt, and as shocked as I felt. I guess she'd expected them to be for her, too.

I frowned, rising slowly. "What do you mean?"

"They're for you. They were delivered for you," she said snappily.

"They're probably a thank you from a client."

"Oh, yeah. That makes sense."

Like my receiving flowers from anyone else wouldn't?

"Here, take them." She shoved them into my arms and left. It was a beautiful arrangement of red roses and white calla lilies.

It better not be from that Mike Crawford. He's married.

As I plucked the card off the plastic stick, I had another thought. Surely, they're not from Greg, and that's why Michelle's upset. Maybe he thought he could schmooze me into spying on our rival firm. Or maybe he wanted something else... I shivered and hurriedly slid the card out from the envelope.

TO THANK YOU, IN PART, FOR HELPING ME LAST NIGHT. THE SECOND PART OF MY THANK YOU WOULD BE...TAKING YOU TO DINNER TONIGHT? LET ME KNOW IF YOU'RE AVAILABLE. -NICK

A phone number was written in the margin. I took in a slow, deep breath and tried to calm the rapid beat of my heart and the little flutter in my stomach.

I mean, the flowers are gorgeous, and the man who sent them is, too.

A knock on the door made me jump and press the card to my chest. I spun, and Greg Zonderbond was letting himself into my office.

"Can I help you?"

He smiled toothily. "Who are the flowers from?"

"A friend. Is that all you needed?"

He frowned. "I'd like to see the Rathford file, please."

"Rathford file?" I circled my desk, taking my card with me so that he wouldn't see it. I sat at my computer, setting the card facedown before grabbing my mouse. "I can send it to you."

"Oh, not the electronic file," he said quickly. "The paperwork."

"Why would you have to see the paperwork on one of my cases?"

"I'm just checking something."

That was vague.

"What on earth would you be checking?"

"I understand we're missing a signature."

I stood and went to my filing cabinet. "I can assure you—" Catching movement out of the corner of my vision I whirled.

He had picked up my card and was reading it. I charged at him. "That's my private correspondence." I tried to take it from him, but he held it beyond my reach.

"This is my office, and any correspondence sent here is mine."

"I don't think that's how it works."

A grin slid across his face as he read, and he studied me. "You do quick work."

I attempted to get it again, and this time managed to seize it, walking behind my desk with it. "This is merely a thank you," I said, trying to sound dismissive.

"No. It's *part* of a thank you. The other part is dinner, and then a nightcap at his place, after which he will lead you to the bedroom and show you how truly thankful he is."

I ground my teeth but didn't say anything.

He sauntered around my desk. I retreated from him, but my desk was against the wall so there was no place to go. "You told me yesterday you wouldn't seduce him." He leaned forward and gripped the back of my chair. "I guess you're one of those girls who says no when they really mean yes."

I wouldn't let him know how much my pulse was racing with fear. I forced myself to look him in the eye. "Get out of my office."

His jaw tightened. "Did you forget I'm your boss?"

"Did you forget what the definition of sexual harassment is?"

He laughed but returned to the other side of my desk. Acting like he was smelling my flowers, he instead plucked one of the rose buds from its stem and smashed it in his fist. Staring at me, he opened his hand one finger at a time, and petals floated down onto my desk calendar, and, finally, the rest of the destroyed bloom landed with a *thump*. He planted his fists on my desk and leaned toward me. "Keep up the good work, Barbara Jean."

I simply glared at him, so angry I was shaking.

He turned around and left, closing the door quietly behind him but looking back at me with a sick grin on his face.

I spent the rest of my day, on company time, updating my resume, because I was getting away from my firm as soon as I could.

CHAPTER SEVEN

Nick

I read the text message again.

HI, NICK. THIS IS B.J. THANK YOU FOR THE FLOWERS. THEY ARE GORGEOUS. ABOUT DINNER TONIGHT—I DON'T THINK THAT'S SUCH A HOT IDEA, SEEING AS WE WORK FOR COMPETING FIRMS. AND THERE'S NO REASON TO THANK ME ANYWAY. -B.J.

The first two sentences sounded in my head like they were spoken by the voice of Coed B.J. The rest I heard in her cool, crisp Lawyer B.J. tone. Or maybe it was B.J. in the courtroom, Barbara Jean at home. I set my phone on my desk and leaned back in my chair.

So, I guess that's the end of that. Maybe she's not as attracted to me as I am to her.

I was antsy. I got up and walked over to one of the long windows which had a phenomenal view of the Rockies.

At least I know now that I can feel something. Feel something for someone who isn't Zoe.

I liked the person I was with Zoe. With her, I was less of a jerk. Still a jerk but less of one. And maybe, one day, I wouldn't have been one at all.

It shouldn't take Zoe in your life to grow and change, Nick.

But that's simply how it was. Even as far back as grade school. If I was happy, I felt I had enough contentment to share with others. When I wasn't happy, I treated people like crap. And I think I was worse whenever I was with Zack and Zoe. I could tell, long before Zack caught on, that Zoe was into him. Maybe it was because I was into her. If it was only Zack and I, I was better. I sighed. I'd had eight years that I'd been ruthless, driven to accumulate things to impress her. Without her in those years, I had used people, especially women. But I'd done some mean shit to guys too. Like my friend Gabe. I'd forever ruined that relationship when I stole his girl, just because I could, and it made me feel slightly less unhappy. In my mind's eye, I retraced the years, all the faces of the people I'd hurt.

All because I didn't have Zoe? What a shitty way to live.

And that's when I decided that I didn't want to live like that anymore. I'd been miserable to others and miserable on the inside. The months I'd been with Zoe were the happiest days of my life. The days when I'd been better to people because I wanted to be a better man for her. Maybe it was time to reclaim that man for myself.

I focused on the people walking the streets below me.

Look what you've done, B.J. McCaffrey. You've changed me, and you weren't even trying. It's too bad you wouldn't give me the chance to discover who we could be together.

It felt like a weight had been lifted. Maybe I wasn't chained to that version of Nick I didn't like. I knew I wouldn't wake up tomorrow and be some kind of choir boy. Old habits and all that. But at least I could work on being better each day.

I decided one way to do that was to call my mom. In my years climbing the corporate ladder, I hadn't given her the time she deserved. I had gone to see her, maybe once every six to eight weeks. But I could do better. Only now she was in an Alzheimer's ward at home in Lincoln, getting worse with each passing day. Some days she didn't know me. It was painful, and I'd thought about never going back. But even though she might not know me, I always knew and loved her, and so I continued visiting her. I sat at my desk, dialed the number, and she answered, her voice sounding older than the last time I'd called—a week ago.

"Hi, Mama."

"Who is this?" she said, suspicion lacing her words.

Turning parallel to the desk, I bent, rubbing my forehead with a sigh, acknowledging the small stab of pain it gave me and moving on. "It's Nickie, Mama." We had been tight. Dad had left when I was ten, and it'd been just the two of us.

"Nickie...?"

I waited for her to search her brain, hoping she'd come up with some memory of me.

Yes, Nickie. Your son.

"Oh, Nickie," she said with more assurance. "I didn't recognize your voice."

I never knew if she was faking it or not, but I liked to think that she still knew me, a little anyway. "How have you been?"

"Oh, you know. Same ol' same ol'."

It was always her response. At least she was happy. I knew that sometimes Alzheimer patients were angry, and I didn't fool myself into thinking that might not happen to her. "Have you been playing any bridge?" It amazed me that she didn't know who I was but could remember every rule of bridge. In fact, she could practically recall every hand she'd ever had and tell you where she'd made a mistake.

"Oh, yes."

It made me smile. "Winning?"

"Of course. You know me, son—" So she did remember me. She sounded better now. More focused. "—I don't hold with any of that losing."

I chuckled. "No. I don't guess you do." Maybe I'd gotten my ruthlessness from her. "You've been taking it easy on those old people though, haven't you?"

"Taking it easy? No way. I'm as old as they are. They deserve none of my mercy. How have you been, Nickie? How's Zoe?"

Mom loved Zoe. Everybody loved Zoe. "I'm not with Zoe anymore, remember?" I said gently. "She married Zack."

"Oh, yes. I forgot." She sounded sad.

"Uhh...I've been good." Liar. "I think I might be ready to date again." Like really date, not just sleep with people; but I wasn't telling her that.

"Oh?"

"Yeah. I think it's time."

"Good for you, Nickie."

We had a nice conversation, but after a bit, I could tell she was getting tired. "Well, I've got to go, Mom." My voice turned soft. "You take care of yourself." I pulled up my calendar on my computer, finding a free weekend and adding a trip to Lincoln. "I'll be down soon to see you."

"Okay, kid."

I knew she'd slipped and forgotten me. She called everyone kid when she couldn't remember their name.

"I love you."

"I love you, too," she said automatically.

"Bye now."

I listened for her, "Bye-bye," and disconnected.

I glanced at the time on my computer screen and decided to knock off early. I'd put in some work later at home.

I was running to the Denver Animal Shelter, about four miles from my office. It had seemed the most pleasant option for community service to meet Judge Walter's demands. I pulled my Maserati into a parking spot, deciding to sell it, and two of my other vehicles. I didn't need them. One was sufficient.

The lady at the desk ran over the rules with me and showed me around. "You can start by taking Bruno for a walk."

Bruno was a graying German Shepherd with sad, soulful eyes. "That's it?" I said, surprised. "You're letting me go on my own?"

"It's not brain surgery, Mr. Adams."

I decided now was as good a time as any to try being nice. "It's Nick."

"Okay. Nick. You remember where the leashes are?"

I nodded.

"He'll need a good fifteen minutes of exercise, if you can spare us that."

"You've got it."

She left.

I gazed at my new friend. "So, Bruno. I guess it's just you and me. I'll be back in a second." I went to get a leash, but when I returned, I heard a familiar voice.

"Yes, you're such a good girl, Blanche," she cooed.

I circled to the other side of the cages to confirm my guess. I was right—it was B.J., of all people. She was sitting crisscross inside a cage with what looked like a mophead with eyes. She had an Avalanche ball cap on, a slick ponytail sticking out the rear, and was wearing faded jeans and an oversized sweatshirt. She still was hot. "What are you doing here? Get on Walters's bad side?"

She blinked at me in surprise, setting the mophead on the floor and starting to get to her feet. I reached to help her up. "No. Not everyone is forced into community service, Adams. Some of us do it because we like it." She leaned in, and I caught a whiff of her perfume, which smelled expensive—if that was possible—classy, and sophisticated. "But don't tell people. I have a reputation to maintain."

I tugged on the bill of her hat. "Your secret's safe with me. Who's this little guy?" I bent to pet the squirming furball at my feet, a tad concerned that in his excitement he would pee on my obnoxiously expensive Christian Louboutin shoes. I still had on my work clothes. He gave a few friendly yaps, which were greeted with similar yips, howls, and some deep barks down the line.

She bent too, and it was like I didn't exist anymore. The pup was all about B.J. "This is Blanche, and she's a sweetheart."

"Do you want to walk together?"

She looked around. "Who are you taking?"

"Bruno."

"Sure. Bruno and Blanche get along well."

It hadn't occurred to me that some dogs wouldn't play well with others. I had a lot to learn. "Here, you take this leash, and I'll get another one."

She was at Bruno's cage when I got there, and Bruno seemed to know and share the same high opinion of B.J. that Blanche did. The depression had vanished from his eyes, and his tail was wagging.

"I see Bruno knows you."

"Yes, he does," she said, giving him a kiss on the head as I hooked the leash in my hands to his collar.

The dogs sniffed each other. "Let's go, buddy," I told Bruno, and we ambled toward the door. I twisted to look at her. "How long have you been coming here?"

"Umm...since I moved to Denver...seven or eight years."

"Wow. That's commitment."

She shrugged. "I never had pets growing up. We could barely feed ourselves, let alone any animals."

I began to realize I didn't know B.J. McCaffrey at all. "Where are you from?"

"Harlan, Kentucky."

"Kentucky, huh? You don't have an accent."

She checked traffic before we crossed the street. "I worked very hard to get rid of it." When I continued to stare at her, she added, "People don't respect you if you talk like a hick." She ended her sentence with a full Kentucky twang.

I gawked. "That didn't just come from your mouth."

She laughed. "Yes, it did."

I was happy she was opening up to me now. "You know, you're pretty amazing."

Her laughter slowed, and she eyed me warily. "What? Because I can talk like a hillbilly?"

"No." I dared to reach over and squeeze her hand. She looked away, and I thought I blew it. "Because you changed yourself. Made something of yourself. I've been thinking of making some changes of my own."

She whirled to observe me. "You have?"

I shrugged, kicking a rock along the sidewalk. "I don't know. I recently got out of a relationship."

"With Zoe?"

I blinked. "Did we talk about this?"

"Sort of," she said evasively. I let an uncomfortable silence descend, staring at her until she added, "Well, you did. I think you were...dreaming of her."

I bobbed my head. "Ahh." I winced and became quiet.

"Can I ask you a question?" she said tentatively.

I squinted into the setting sun, dragging in a breath. I guess I'd brought this on. I didn't really feel like discussing Zoe, but I didn't want the conversation to end.

"Sure."

"You don't have to," she said quickly.

"No. I want to." I grinned at her sideways. "Give it to me."

"Why does my boss hate you so much?"

I chuckled. "That's what you want to know?"

"Yes. It seems a bit excessive."

"Mmm." I looked around, forming my answer. "Greg and I went to law school together. There was this girl..."

She smirked. "Always a girl."

"True. Greg and I were both dating her, but neither one of us knew about the other."

She grimaced. "Ooh. Ouch."

"Yeah. I got over it. I guess he never did."

We walked farther while she thought. "What was her name?" she asked offhandedly.

"Sarah."

"Sarah? As in Sarah Zonderbond? Greg's wife?"

I didn't turn my head. "Yep."

"You slept with his wife?"

My lips lifted. "I didn't say that."

"But you slept with her."

I glanced at her. "I plead the fifth on that one, counselor."

She gasped, her gaze wide when she looked at me.

I laughed. "They weren't married at the time."

She smiled, too, peering ahead as I had. "No wonder he hates you."

I gestured, unintentionally pulling Bruno away from a patch of grass with an interesting smell. "What? I'm a pretty nice guy."

She rolled her eyes. We'd circled around and ended up at the shelter. She paused outside of the door. "That's not what I heard."

I frowned. "Sic her, Bruno."

Bruno sat contemplating us, wagging his tail.

I leaned in and put a hand to my mouth to "whisper" to Bruno. "You're making me look bad, boy." He panted, cocked his head, and continued to wag his tail. "Man's best friend, my ass."

She giggled, her face bright.

I studied my feet for a moment then shifted my gaze to hers. "You're beautiful when you smile, you know."

Her smile dimmed a fraction, and in her eyes, I saw something I'd never seen in the courtroom. Fear. Or maybe fear was too strong, but it was definitely more than unease. She was always so in control in the courtroom. Scary, even. But that was not what I was seeing now. She blinked a couple of times, and the sentence held in the air. Then she recovered.

"Oh, sure. Wearing my hat and sweatshirt..."

"Your beauty flows from within." Where did that come from?

She stared at me then scoffed. "Oh, right." She turned and opened the door. "That's a Nick Adams come-on if I ever heard one."

I laughed. "No. I'm serious."

"Yeah, yeah."

She returned Blanche to her pen, and I squared Bruno away. I called over the cages. "So, Miss Pro, what do I do now?"

She showed me the laundry room for dog and cat beds and blankets, and the sinks where the food and water bowls were cleaned, and we went to work. After an hour and a half, we decided we'd put in our due. I walked out with her.

"That your Maserati?"

I'd always felt so proud to show it to a girl. Now I felt ashamed. What had changed? I hung my head a little. "Yeah."

"Wow. Nice."

"Yeah, it's a bit extravagant."

"Guess which one's mine."

I pointed to a modest sedan.

"Nope." She moved forward a step or two and put her arm on the hood of the Cadillac Escalade in front of us. A maxed-out Cadillac Escalade. I'd priced them. She'd paid at least a hundred-fifty grand to have the privilege of driving it.

"Well, well."

She leaned in, and I caught another whiff of her perfume, which had come to drive me crazy. "They pay us far too much, don't they?" We laughed. Neither of us got in our cars.

"You know...we've spent a good portion of the afternoon together...what could one little dinner hurt?"

Her mouth hung open for a moment. She peered at the setting sun, and I prepared myself for a rejection. She shifted her gaze to me, and I felt a shiver of desire. "You have a point," she said slowly. I was riveted on how good her lips looked and almost lost her response.

"So, you'll go with me?" I wished I didn't sound so much like a dweeby middle schooler getting permission to go on his first date with the head cheerleader.

"I'd need to take a shower..."

"Not a problem," I assured her. "I can pick you up at seven."

"That'll work." She went to get behind the wheel, and I turned to cross to mine. She called, "Adams!" I twisted around. She was standing on her footboard, one arm on her roof, the other on the top of her open door. "Where are you taking me?"

"How about Guard and Grace?"

"Perfect. See you at seven."

I got in my car and talked to my dashboard. "I have a date with B.J. McCaffrey. Bizarre." But I was thrilled.

CHAPTER EIGHT

Nick

I now know where the term hubba hubba comes from, because when she opened the door, all I could struggle out was, "Hu-hu-hu-hu..." then I gave up on speech altogether. I had meant to say hello, but I couldn't get any air behind my words because my lungs were suddenly depleted of it. Her dress...she...it all was amazing. The dress was black, and the top was held together by a silver metal rectangle between her breasts. The bottom of the rectangle ran through a loop in the skirt portion of the dress, leaving some of her midriff bare. It was sexy as hell, yet also, somehow, elegant. It hugged her hips and...what it did for her...I was not worthy of viewing. She wore it with the ease and confidence that she brought into the courtroom. I stared for a long moment then shook my head to clear it and swallowed to loosen my throat.

"I'm sorry. Hello. Good evening."

"Hi."

I didn't move.

"Umm...are you ready to go?"

"Oh. Yes. Yes." I scooted back so she could exit, and she locked her door.

She slipped the key into her purse, which was small, black, and sequined, the straps made up of a number of silver rectangles that matched the one on her dress.

"Nick? Are you okay?"

I had spaced out. We'd gone from her place, down the hall, in the elevator, and to the lobby, and I didn't remember any of it. I'd been affected by Zoe at times, but, in the end, it was Zoe. A known entity. Familiar. The gal I'd played basketball with on the driveway. B.J. was new. Mysterious. Phenomenal. And the more I discovered about her, the more I craved her. Legal shark B.J., coed B.J., the caring person she was at the shelter, and whoever else was in there. It excited me to know that I might have the opportunity to explore other facets of her.

I smiled at her. "Perfect."

Because I tipped them generously, the valets had held my Maserati in front. When the guy handed me the keys, I slipped him another hunny.

"Oh, no, sir. You already paid us."

Honest lad. I'll have to remember him.

I opened the door for B.J. as I told him. "That's for not taking my baby for a ride."

The guy grinned. "I was tempted." He nodded. "Thanks."

"No problem." I always felt like people in service positions deserved my money more than I. Of course, sometimes I did it to impress a woman. I cocked my head thinking about it. Not tonight. I guess I didn't feel the need to impress B.J. Or maybe I knew she wouldn't be impressed and would see right through me. "Are you up for a drink at 54thirty before dinner?"

She gave my arm a quick squeeze. "That sounds nice."

Hmm...maybe she's down for some physical contact. I know I'm down for physical contact. But I also want to take it slow. Enjoy the buildup.

Which was something new, too.

I need to not jump too fast. I don't want a rebound relationship. I want something...more. Whoa!

I was rushing things, and I knew it. Still... At the next light, I captured her hand for a moment. "I'm glad you decided to come."

"I'm glad I did, too."

I took her to a rooftop bar where they had fire pit tables, couches, and a great view of both the mountains and the city. It was busy, and we threaded our way through the crowd, searching for tables. We came to a table that was roped off, with a reserved sign.

"I don't think there are any tables," she said, craning her neck. "But maybe we can find someplace to at least stand and lean."

"What about this one?"

She glanced back. "It's reserved."

"Is it?" I unhooked the rope and moved it aside.

"Nick," she hissed. "They'll make us leave."

I sat and patted the couch next to me. "Come sit by me."

She peered over her shoulder, going into full panic mode. "Nick, the waiter is coming. Get out of there!"

At that moment, the waiter passed her, and she cringed, looking at me with desperation in her eyes.

"Mr. Adams. Good to see you. I see you found your table."

"Yes, thanks, Max."

"You turkey!" B.J. screamed, coming at me.

I laughed. "What?"

She kneeled on the couch, awkwardly because of the dress she had on, and swatted me mercilessly.

I ducked and blocked the blows. "Stop."

She held up enough to say, "I thought I would have to keep you from being arrested again."

Max gazed at me with raised brows.

"It's a long story." I grabbed her wrists. "Woman!"

She flopped onto her keester with a huff, crossing her arms, but I knew she wasn't really mad.

Max cleared his throat. "Can I get you something to drink, madam?"

"Yes." She still pouted. "Give me the most expensive thing on the menu. He needs to be punished."

Max looked at me.

I was still laughing. "You heard the lady. I'll take a Manhattan."

"Yes, sir." He spun to leave, and B.J. grabbed his pant leg.

"I'm just kidding. But I will have a glass of champagne. The cheapest you have."

"Are you sure?" I asked her. "You can get whatever you want. In all seriousness."

"Positive. I don't like expensive champagne. I like cheap champagne."

"Good to know."

Max left.

She didn't say anything.

"B.J.," I wheedled.

She huffed and turned her back to me, crossing her arms again.

"Are you really mad?"

Again, she ignored me, twisting more and raising her chin with a big exhale.

I swept her hair over her shoulder. I was ninety-nine percent sure she was messing with me. "Come on." I bent to speak in her ear. "I'm sorry. I'll make it up to you." I felt her shiver in response, and I sighed.

I've still got it.

She whirled and gave me a sexy smile. "Now you're talking, Adams." She ran her painted fingernails along my jaw, leaning in.

I tilted my head to receive her kiss, turned on to the max.

"Nick?" Her warm breath played on my lips. Her hand was on my thigh and sliding closer to certain important areas. "You're..."

Yes? Yes?

"...a big jerk." She sat back triumphantly.

I groaned, shutting my eyes.

"You don't play fair," I rasped out.

She laughed.

Max arrived and presented her with a flute.

"Thank you, Max."

I was still grimacing, in a sort of exquisite pain.

"Are you all right, Mr. Adams?"

"No. I am not all right. I am definitely not all right."

B.J. laughed harder.

"I'll take that drink now." I gave B.J. a faux glare. "I need it."

When Max left, I had my arm on the back of the couch. A cold wind blew off the mountains, and B.J. set her flute on the table and snuggled into my side.

"Ooh. I'm cold."

"Do you want to go inside?"

"No, no," she said quickly. "I like it right here."

I grunted, pretending to still be miffed. I studied her. As close as she was, it was awkward but worth the effort. She was staring out at the mountains, so I did, too. The dark outline of the hills looked like a giant, curled up on his side, taking a nap.

"It's a beautiful night," she murmured.

I peered at her again. "Yes, it is." We sat peacefully for a moment. I ran my hand along her shoulder, relishing the feel of her skin. "You have a playful side."

"I guess I do," she said thoughtfully.

A couple of guys walked by, and one ran his gaze over her. I instinctively drew her tighter.

"I don't show it to many people," she murmured.

"I feel privileged." My voice came out husky.

She smiled at me brightly. "You should." Then she looked at the mountains again. "I can't be soft in the courtroom. I have to maintain my reputation as a hard ass," she added wistfully.

Sounds like a pretty solitary, lonely life.

"I didn't know I was hanging around a lady with a reputation," I joked.

She elbowed me lightly and sat up to get her drink. "It's not like you had one to tarnish," she teased back, but it kind of hit me hard.

Levelling my gaze at the Rockies, I thought about my life. The choices I'd made. I'd been doing that a lot lately. Without Zoe, I was adrift, at a crossroads. Where did I go from here?

"You're quiet."

I drank, too. "I've made a lot of poor choices in my life. I constructed this kind of ideal picture of what I wanted from life and worked to achieve that."

When I paused to formulate my next sentence, she interjected. "I don't think that's necessarily a bad thing..."

"No. I suppose not. But I was focused on the wrong goals." I looked at her. "I think I'm ready to make some changes."

She searched my face with that penetrating gaze that made witnesses fall apart on the stand, and I felt like she could read everything in my features. "Why is that?"

I held my tumbler in my hand with one finger extended across the rim. I turned a bit as I answered, not wanting her to see too much. "You, in part."

"Me?" she said, wide-eyed.

"Yeah. I saw you there at the shelter, volunteering your time, and it made me think."

We sat with that for a moment.

"Tell me about Zoe."

It seemed to come out of the blue, but yet, it didn't. Zoe was part of the conversation. I sighed. "Zoe." Just saying her name made me a little emotional. "I've known Zoe forever. We grew up together. My best friend, Zack, lived next door to her, and the three of us hung around together constantly. ZNZ like DDT, Zoe used to say."

Her brow furrowed as if puzzling over that.

"Zack, Nick, and Zoe."

"That sounds nice."

"It was." *Was.* I exhaled the pain.

"What happened?"

I shrugged and sat forward, taking my arm from her shoulder. It was hard to discuss. I drank again then held my glass between my legs, staring into it. "I don't know. We got older..." I finished my drink and rid myself of the glass. "Zoe always had a thing for Zack. I always had a thing for Zoe, although she couldn't see it. I guess her eyes were too full of stars from looking at Zack." Okay, I guess there was still a little bitterness.

"That must have been hard."

I nodded. "It was. But I would joke it off. I was a big joker back then." I hesitated to tell her the rest. "Zack finally got wise and started dating Zoe, and they were in love. Anyone could see it. I could see it. I tried to be happy for them, but..." I lifted my hands then let them fall into my lap. "I loved her. So, when Zack was ready to go to college—he was a year older than us—I thought, this could be my shot. Maybe I could make Zoe...I don't know...love me in return, I guess. I regret what happened next...but I also don't. I put the idea in Zack's head that if he really cared about Zoe, he would let her go, so that she could enjoy her senior year. Of course, they were both miserable. And for eight years, I waited for Zoe to get over him, and for me to make myself into someone Zoe would fall for." I sighed. "I became Mr. Big Shot Lawyer, bought a nice place, cars, expensive clothes...but I didn't get Zoe at all. She didn't want any of that." I became quiet, considering it as I explained it to her. It made it clearer to me.

"You said you regretted it but didn't regret it. What did you mean?"

That was the lawyer in her. She had me on the stand and was drawing out the information she needed. But I didn't mind. She was a good listener.

"Zoe and I got together, and it was good. Really good. But, in the end, I wasn't Zack. Zack came back and that was the end of Zoe and Nick. Just like that." I looked at her. "I regretted it, because it was an awful thing to do to your friends. I didn't regret it, because I had seven months to show Zoe how much I loved her, and I can't regret that. It was the best time of my life."

She put her hand on mine. "You deserve someone who can love you the way you loved Zoe. It was like you were cramming two puzzle pieces together to make them fit when they weren't meant to, bending their sides as you did it."

I nodded. "I know." I took a deep breath. "So, that's Zoe. But I'm putting that time in my past now." I glanced at my Rolex. "I should probably get the check so we can make our reservation at Guard and Grace."

CHAPTER NINE

B.J.

I would have never imagined there was so much depth to Nick Adams. While he was telling me about his love for Zoe, I was falling in love with him. He was so young when it all started. We all do foolish things when we're young. I know I did. I didn't know Zack, but, in my opinion, Zoe was a fool to let Nick go.

He took me to Guard and Grace, a bougie restaurant/steakhouse with an incredible view. Depending on where diners were seated, they could see the mountains or Denver's skyline. At night, the lights of Denver were very pretty, its own cosmos of twinkling pinpoints, a perfect reflection of the night sky. The food was phenomenal. Ungodly expensive but phenomenal. We both had a steak, since that was their specialty, and I've never had a better steak. For dessert I couldn't decide between the chocolate cake or the sticky toffee cake, so I got the latter, with a chocolate martini.

We dined and discussed law school, some of our more interesting cases, and our favorite things to do in Denver. The conversation continued on the way back to my place but stopped when we got close to the building.

"I'd like to walk you to your door," Nick said carefully.

"Okay." I was suddenly nervous as hell.

In the elevator, as we neared my floor, he held my hand and kissed it. "I had a very nice evening."

We reached my floor and exited. "I did, too."

He accompanied me down the hall. "What would you think about going out again sometime?"

My heart charged forward. "I'm not sure, since we have a case together..."

"We don't. I got myself recused from the case."

What? "On what grounds?"

He stared at his feet. "Mental distress. I'm stepping back for a bit."

"Oh." Was there any reason to say no then?

He laced his fingertips through mine and peered at our hands. "So? Do you think you'd be interested in seeing me again?" He looked up, with a slight grimace.

I pushed onto my tiptoes and gave him a quick kiss. "I'd love to."

His face brightened. "Great. Are you free tomorrow night? Or is that too soon?"

I was filled with warmth. "Tomorrow night would be great."

"Okay. Perfect. What would you like to do?"

"Let's do something more casual this time."

"All right. Casual. I can do that. I'll think about it and text you some ideas." He clapped once. "Awesome. Say...6:30?"

"That works for me."

"I'll text you later."

"Great."

He took my hands. "I guess this is good night then. I look forward to seeing you tomorrow." He nodded his head toward the door. "After I see you in, I'll take off."

"Oh, okay." I unlocked the door and opened it.

He gave me a long, smoldering look. "Good night, B.J." He turned and strode quickly in the opposite direction.

I stirred from the spell he'd put on me with his eyes. "Adams!"

He spun.

"So...no kiss good night?"

He walked slowly toward me, and my heart was in my throat.

"I wasn't sure how you'd feel if I did that."

He was a hair's breadth away. I swallowed, but my voice still came out roughly. "So, now you know. What are you going to do about it?" I smiled, but everything inside of me churned with nerves.

He grinned. "This." He drew me into his strong embrace, tilted his head, his gaze studying me as he lowered his soft, full lips to mine. It was like no other kiss I'd ever had before, but yet, somehow familiar, like our mouths knew what to do together. A rush of sensations filled me.

Oh. This is what it feels like to be kissed by someone who knows what they're doing.

It was both commanding and gentle. Taking mercilessly yet offering in abundance. I gave myself to him completely, holding nothing back, releasing all the safeguards I usually kept tight rein on. When I'd been with any other man, I'd felt uncertain. I analyzed every nuance and worried over what would happen next. I didn't feel that way with Nick. I felt safe and cared for, which was a dangerous thought.

This is Nick Adams. He doesn't care about you. It's all a game with him. You're nothing more than a pawn in his eyes.

That wouldn't normally worry me. I knew how to handle men and could play the game right along with him.

But this didn't feel like a game.

And that scared the shit out of me.

CHAPTER TEN

Nick

My elbows were planted on my desk, fingers folded together, my thumbs resting against my lips as I replayed the kiss that had held me captive all night and all morning long. It had been powerful, moving me to my very core, filling me with desire and something much stronger.

B.J. McCaffrey.

People called her an ice princess. Hell, I'd called her that and worse. But there was no iciness to her, only pure, unadulterated heat. I felt like I'd met my match, and that both thrilled and terrified me.

Someone rapped on the frame of my open door. "Nick?" My partner, Clint McGuire, stood outside with his arm still raised.

"Oh. Come in. Have a seat."

He was a pudgy, sloppy man, his curly hair always awry, beard never properly trimmed, glasses perpetually smudged. He was my antithesis, but under it all was a brilliant legal mind. His nerdy, unmanaged appearance worked to his advantage. No one expected much from him. He set a thermos with a faded plaid, plastic wrapping around it on my desk. "Thinking about a case?"

I tapped on the lid of my Starbuck's cup. "Not really."

He looked me over as he lowered himself into a chair. "No suit? You taking the day off?"

"No. Just thought I'd take some time to catch up on paperwork."

"Huh." He continued to eye me. "Got anything to do with being held in contempt of court yesterday?"

Word gets around quickly.

I shrugged. "Not really. How are things going with Johnny Caine?" I'd told him I wanted to meet with him and discuss the celebrity's case.

He grunted. "He's a piece of work, man."

Johnny Caine, star of stage and screen, was a sex icon on film and had cultivated an intellectual, aloof persona in real life. He made being a drunk seem cool, his hallmark lavish lifestyle so much a part of him it seemed as if he was born wearing shades and smoking a stogie, half in the bottle. And not a bottle of formula, mind you, straight gin. His eccentricities drew people to him like a magnet, although his recent court case had tarnished his image some. His ex-wife was accusing him of beating her senseless when she was pregnant with their only child, who was already a media darling, though not out of diapers yet. Smoky Caine's bowel movements were covered in papers across the world, and her designer onesies had inspired knock-off brands by the dozen.

"Is he really as bizarre as people say?"

Clint nodded vehemently. "Worse. He's paranoid about his privacy, and sometimes I wonder if he's really all there. Ya know what I mean?"

"Huh. I've got to meet this guy."

Clint waved his hands. "Oh, no. He'll speak solely to me. I've assured him that I've kept his information safe, that I haven't even shared it with you or Sheri. He—"

"I get it, Clint. I was saying that more as a general statement. I'm not even really a fan." I leaned back in my chair. "I take it you can only update me on the case in general terms then."

"Yes."

"Then how's it going? Generally."

"Good." He didn't add anything.

"Good? That's all you've got?"

He rose. "Yep."

I watched as he circled his chair. "Well, I'm glad we had this little meeting to fill me in on the case. Keep up the good work," I said sarcastically.

He smiled. "You've got it." And he left.

I shook my head, paging through some papers on my desk. "I'm starting to think Clint is as squirrely as our client."

I worked on paperwork for most of the morning and made a few business calls. When I stopped for lunch, it dawned on me that I didn't have a plan for my date with B.J., and I wracked my brain for something to do. I hadn't done anything "casual" since Zoe. I usually wined and dined my women. The only thing casual about our dates was the sex. And I was pretty sure that wasn't what B.J. was referring to when she said she wanted to do something casual. At the last minute, I thought of something and arrived on her doorstep at exactly 6:30.

She opened the door to my knock. "Hiya, sexy," she said with a grin.

"Hi, yourself. Don't you look cute." She had on a pair of perfectly faded jeans and a Colorado Buffaloes sweatshirt.

She rolled her eyes. "Right." She nudged me out of the way so she could lock the door. "What are we doing?"

"Bowling."

"Bowling? Hmm." She tilted her head with a slight frown.

I tried to read her reaction. "We don't have to do that if you don't want to."

I should have had a backup plan.

"You don't like bowling?" I pushed the button to descend.

"I've never been."

Is that even possible? "Never been?"

She elbowed me lightly as we got into the elevator. "Don't act like I'm some kind of freak. We didn't have money for it when I was little, and I spent all of my free time studying in law school."

"Well...we can do something else if you want..."

"No." She smiled at me. "This'll be fun."

"So, each round you get two rolls to try to knock all the pins down," I explained. "Each frame on the score card represents a player's turn."

"Ahh." She had a finger on her lips.

"Do you understand?"

"Yes."

"Good." I got up to show her how it was done.

"Just one question."

I spun.

"What's a frame?"

"Uhh..." I tried to think through my answer.

"Don't you roll your eyes at me," she snapped playfully.

I chuckled. "What? I didn't roll my eyes."

"Yes, you did. On the inside."

I raised my brows. "On the inside?"

She frowned and crossed her arms. "Just roll your ball, Adams."

I twisted away from her. "That's what I was trying to do," I muttered, amused.

I toed the line, taking a deep breath and concentrating. It'd been a while since I played, and I wanted to do well in front of her. I set up to the left of the center line, as had been my custom, bent my knees, focused on the arrows in the middle of the lane, made my approach, letting my arm swing back as I stepped and bringing it forward, making sure to follow through. I was rewarded when the ball hit the pocket, and I heard that wonderful crash that was one solid noise, meaning all the pins would be falling.

I rotated, struggling to not look too pleased with myself.

"Act like you've been there," Zack always said.

"See? It's easy."

She frowned. "Uh-huh."

"Now. It's your turn."

"But I thought you said you got two balls."

"Well, you do, if you don't knock them all down with the first one, like I did." A little smugness seeped in.

She narrowed her eyes.

I walked her through the motions, then sat to enjoy the show, my fingers laced behind my head. She rolled and stood to watch her ball ride the side of the gutter a couple of feet before falling into it. She continued to stare as if the pins would somehow magically collapse. Her ball wobbled in the gutter until it reached the end.

I tried to encourage her. "That's a good start. Maybe you'll get one on your next turn." I covered a snicker.

She scowled at me, and I coughed, pretending to be concentrating on the scoreboard. When her ball came back, she picked it up wordlessly and repeated her previous steps with the same result.

This'll be a long night.

She peered at the board. "Hey! You gave me two zeros."

"That's because you didn't knock down any pins, sweetheart."

She growled.

"Maybe if you—"

She raised a palm. "I don't need your help. I'm going to the bathroom," she announced.

When she left, I got a spare, glad that she hadn't seen my first ball just nick the seven pin before falling into the gutter. She was gone for a while but reappeared with a determined look on her face. Without saying anything, she marched over to the ball return, grabbed her ball, and got into position. I prepared myself for another gutter ball. She went through the steps, kicking her leg behind her and giving a small hop at the end, and the little shit got a strike. She wiped invisible dust from her hands.

"Your turn," she said sweetly as I sat gaping at her.

"How did you...?"

"Come on. Your ball's getting cold."

I grasped my hips. "You watched YouTube videos in the john, didn't you?"

She grinned. "Maybe I did; maybe I didn't."

"Okay. Okay. Game on."

I won the first game fairly easily. The next was tougher. On the third, she finished off with a turkey to beat me by one stupid-ass pin. She jumped up and down.

"I won. I won!"

I couldn't help but feel a little happy for her. "Yes, you did. Come over here."

When she got close, I pulled her into my lap and kissed her. To my pleasure, she responded in kind, bracketing my face with her hands as she blew my mind.

"Let's go," I said with a rasp.

"My thought exactly."

On the way to her place, we decided to take a bottle of wine to the roof. B.J. said they had a nice patio up there, and it was a beautiful night. While she gathered supplies, I strolled around the living room. Coming to a stop in front of the pedestal with the cowgirl hat on it, I put it on as she exited the kitchen. I stuck out my chest, pretending to loop my thumbs through imaginary suspenders as she walked to me, her lips twitching. "Lady, don't try to resist me," I said in a deep voice, giving it a twang. "I'm a lawman."

She fluttered a hand to her heart, looking at me with wide eyes. "Oh, whatever shall I do?" she said in a fake Southern belle accent.

"Ooh! You do that good," I growled. I took the hat off and placed it on her head. "Your turn to be the law," I challenged.

"Okay. Spin."

"Spin?" I questioned.

She made circles with her finger. "Spin," she insisted.

Hesitantly, I did what she said. The next thing I knew, she was on my back, digging the heels of her boots into me.

"Giddy-up, little doggie."

I laughed. "Ouch. That hurts. And, I'll have you know, there ain't nothin' little about my doggie."

"Ooh," she moaned.

I ducked a shoulder and swung her down to the floor, drawing her in by her hips and kissing her. The kisses were deep and sultry, and when my body started to respond to them, I pulled away, laying my forehead on hers and closing my eyes as I exhaled.

"Let's go upstairs," she said.

She led the way, and we were glad to find it empty when we opened the door at the top. It was nice. There were fire pits and potted plants, conversation areas marked by rugs with sofas and seats, lights swagged under umbrellas, and they even had a hammock in one corner. We sat and talked, drank wine and ate some cheese, crackers, nuts, chocolate, and grapes, our bowling alley hamburgers and fries having worn off. I slouched in the corner of one couch, and she leaned against me as we stared at the skies, pointing constellations out to each other. Our fingers were entwined, and I raised them, the moon highlighting some small, white, jagged scars.

"How did you get these?"

"Oh. Those are ugly." She tried to snatch her hand away, but I held on.

I brought it to my lips and kissed it. "They are not. They're part of you, and that makes them beautiful."

She blinked and didn't comment at first. "My dad came after me with a broken beer bottle."

I wasn't expecting that. "Really? Why?"

She shrugged. "He was drunk."

My brow furrowed. "Did that happen often?"

"The drinking, yes. The coming after me...not often."

I was quiet, mulling that over. She sat suddenly and looked at me earnestly. "He's not a bad man, though. He just...after Mama died, he started to drink a lot."

I don't think she was even aware that her Kentucky accent had snuck into her words as she spoke of home. "How old were you when your mother died?"

"Eight."

I drew a long breath. I couldn't imagine growing up without my mother. "That's rough."

"Yeah." She leaned forward to grab a cracker and slather some cheese on it. "Do you want one?"

"Yes, thanks."

She gave me the one she'd made and prepared another for herself.

"How did it happen? If you don't mind talking about it..."

"Well...my father worked in the coal mines, but it was my mother who developed lung cancer. She wasn't a smoker, so my father blamed himself, and the coal dust he brought home with him in his clothes. No matter how much baking soda and vinegar she used on them, they were never truly clean. But it wasn't only in his clothes, it was in the air. I never knew what sunshine looked like or breathed fresh air before I ran away."

"You ran away?"

She nodded. "A lot of us did. Kids of coal miners. It was a harsh life, and many of us would rather take our chances on the road than be smothered in that town." She laid her head down in my lap, staring at the stars, her hands folded on her stomach. "One by one my older siblings disappeared, taking off in the middle of the night and never being heard of again. I was the last and stayed much longer than I probably should have." Her voice caught, and she closed her eyes. "Just speaking of it..." She stopped, and I could feel her take a deep, shaky breath. "It's like I can still feel the weight of that air."

Listening to her talk, it was like I could taste the dust and metal on my tongue and feel my throat constricting.

"But all I've been doing is talking about me. We never discuss you," she said with forced brightness.

"Last night the topic of conversation was me and Zoe," I reminded her.

"Oh, yeah." She thought on that for a moment, then sat and worked her way onto my lap. She stroked my face, hers still lined with pain, her brows knit, eyes watery. "Let's not talk then." She kissed me, and my arms automatically tightened around her.

Things quickly became hot and heavy. Her hands were under my lightweight sweater, dipping into my waistband in the back. I caressed her above her clothing at first, but as she pressed into me, molding her hot little body against mine, melting our edges like she was doing her welding and sealing us together, I found her smooth, velvety skin, and all I wanted was more of her.

I kissed her neck, and she moaned.

"We should probably stop."

I didn't comment, holding her more possessively, my actions becoming more heated and urgent. I sunk my teeth into her.

"Oh." The word slid out of her, elongated and breathy. She shifted, rising up to straddle me and whipping her sweatshirt off, throwing it somewhere behind her.

It was incredibly hot, going at it like that, bathed in the lights of the city. She frantically tugged at my shirt, and I broke away enough to rid myself of it. Her hands were everywhere, and every bit of me came alive under them. I lifted her by the waist a little, and she seemed to understand what I wanted her to do, shimmying down under me as I stretched above her. I writhed against her, and she arched into me, digging her nails into my back.

"I want you," I growled, irritated that the wicker couch didn't give me enough room to maneuver the way I desired to. The cool mountain air made her nipples hard as I skimmed my thumbs over her bra. I yanked the fabric aside and sucked on her nipple. She made a high-pitched cry, rising to press into me even more.

A *slam* and the loud screech of metal made me raise my head.

"Oh, shit!" Wide-eyed, the teenaged boy coming through the door put it in reverse, ramming into the people behind him.

"What?" I heard someone ask.

"Move, move, move," he shouted with a panicked laugh. "There's someone up there."

"Shit," she repeated, pushing on me. "Nick..."

I extended my arm, giving her room, and she rolled from under me. She would have fallen onto the rooftop had I not latched onto her and helped lower her to the carpet. "Did they see anything?" She was laughing.

"No. But I think they got the general picture of what was going on." I reached for my sweater as she scrambled for her clothing.

She grinned. "You're going to get me into trouble."

"Me?" I pulled my shirt over my head. When I popped out of the neck opening, she already had her sweatshirt covering her and was struggling to get into the sleeves.

She sashayed across to me. "You're a bad influence."

"I wasn't the one who—"

She frowned.

"Okay. You're right. I'm a bad influence."

She dragged me in by my hips. "Now you're learning." She lowered her gaze. "I guess we should get going."

"Yes." I sighed. "I guess we should." I began to help her pick up the food. "Too bad, though," I said, looking at her out of the corners of my eyes.

"Damn shame, is what it is."

I chuckled and embraced her, kissing her on her forehead. "Come on."

"Do you think they're down there?"

I cracked the door open. "It's quiet."

She exhaled. "Good. That would be so embarrassing."

We traversed the stairs and when we got to the bottom and opened the door to her hall, four teenaged boys were huddled together, laughing.

"Hi," B.J. said, pretending we weren't the couple they'd seen half-clad on the roof, but the food was a dead giveaway.

"Hey," one of them said, running his gaze over her. I gave him a hard stare as B.J. opened the door.

I helped her put things away then trapped her against the counter. "What do you say we finish what we started upstairs?"

She had her arms between us and was fiddling with one of the three buttons on my sweater.

"I...don't think so."

Damn.

My disappointment must have shown on my face.

"Nick, I'd like to take this slow."

It seemed an odd statement after what just happened.

"That is," she glanced down, "if you were interested in more than a one-night stand."

I liked how she put it out there. She fixed her gaze on me. She had these ice-blue, penetrating eyes that really destroyed me. I swallowed. "I'd like to see where this goes, if you're interested?" I said carefully, not wanting to overcommit if she didn't feel the same.

She slid her hands behind my neck, playing with my hair. "I'm very interested."

"Mmm." I kissed her again, trying to get her engine going, but after a few fantastic kisses, she pulled back.

"Nick, we've got all the time in the world."

I sighed.

Damn kids messed this up for me.

I made an attempt to recover. "Ya know...one of us could get hit by a car tomorrow, and we'll never know what it might have been like..."

She snorted. "Does that work with other women?"

I took a breath to answer, and she put a finger on my lips. "Don't answer. I don't want to know."

I chuckled and looked to the heavens. "You're really going to make me work for this, aren't you?"

She grinned. "Uh-huh."

I exhaled. "Okay. But you'll be the one suffering. Ask any woman I've ever f—" I stopped myself before saying something that would have definitely earned me a slap. "—found attractive and...been intimate with."

She rolled her eyes. "Are you really that impressed with yourself?"

I held my hands up. "It has nothing to do with me being impressed with myself. I'm only stating the facts."

She crossed her arms, still unconvinced.

"Well...I suppose it's time to go then."

Her mouth twitched. "Not without this." She pushed me against the wall, and holding the sides of my face, gave me the most incredible, most wicked kiss of my life. When she backed away from me, I staggered forward, completely undone by her. She smirked, grabbed me by the shoulders, and led me to the door. "Sweet dreams, Nick." Pushing onto her toes, she nibbled on my lower lip one last time and shoved me out the door, laughing.

"Wait," I yelled before she could shut the door. "Dinner tomorrow?"

"Sure," she said immediately.

"Where?"

She thought briefly. "Do you want to go to Bezel?"

It was a swanky place nearby. "Sounds good."

"Why don't you meet me there? I'll get reservations," she offered. "Six?"

I considered insisting that, as the male, I should make the reservations but decided it really didn't matter who did, as long as they were made. "That'll work."

"See you tomorrow then," she said softly and closed the door.

I never would have imagined me and B.J. going at it on the roof of her apartment building. But I knew, no matter what happened to us, I'd be dreaming about this night for years to come. Even if I ended up with someone else, what happened between us would haunt me in a most pleasant way.

Reluctant to leave, and half hoping she'd run after me and tell me she'd changed her mind and wanted me to stay the night, I ambled slowly toward the elevator. So, when I heard her door open, and the pad of her feet rushing toward me, my heartbeat accelerated.

"Nick!"

I turned.

She slowed, walking now and holding my phone out. "You forgot this silly."

"Hmm." I acted like I was reaching for the phone but took her wrist instead and yanked her to me. "That's because I was a bit distracted by this beautiful woman." I gave her a kiss to rival the one she'd given me.

She pulled away with a sigh, and I thought I had her. "You're still not staying over."

I smiled. "Damn."

She traced my jawline. "Although if anything would have changed my mind, it would have been that kiss."

We stood there for a moment, staring into each other's eyes and relishing the charge of electricity that hung in the air.

"Good night, Nick."

"Good night, B.J." I kissed her tenderly one last time and watched her as she strolled away. The elevator dinged open before she reached her door. I would have waited until she got into her place, enjoying the sway of her hips, and the way her black hair swished behind her, but people were on board. I got in, standing in front of the doors, grinning.

The girl had me. Hook, line, and sinker.

CHAPTER ELEVEN

B.J.

I was distracted with thoughts of Nick and so wasn't paying as close attention to my surroundings as I should have been. I'd left my door half open when I left. As I entered, someone followed me and pushed me inside.

I whirled. "What the hell are you doing here?"

Greg Zonderbond was shutting the door behind him. He pivoted and stared at me in a way that made a chill race up my spine. "Is that a way to greet your boss?"

I steeled myself. "Boss or no, you have no right to force yourself into my home."

He moved forward, and I involuntarily retreated, almost missing the steps to the living room. His eyes gleamed. "Do I make you nervous, Barbara Jean?"

"Not at all," I said quickly, but we both knew it was a lie. "What are you doing here?"

He continued advancing on me, walking slowly, deliberately down the stairs. "I came to check on my favorite employee."

I backed up until my legs hit a side table, and I had to react quickly to keep a lamp from crashing to the floor. Pissed that his attempts to intimidate me were working, I spit out, "What do you want, Greg?"

"Hmm. What do I want?" With each word he drew nearer. This time I was able to resist the urge to flee. He closed the gap between us; I held my chin up. He ran a finger along my arm. "I think you are aware of what I want." He grabbed me, hauling me against his body and brushing his lips against my neck. I felt his erection, and my stomach rolled. I knew he got off on frightening me, but the physical evidence of that made me sick.

"You need to leave," I said more steadily than I thought I'd be able to. He pulled away slowly, and when we were eye to eye, I added, "Now."

He tilted his head, smirking, still gripping my biceps.

Is he really not leaving?

My panic rose, and I desperately tried to remember where my phone was. I felt my rear pocket and was glad to find it at my fingertips. I removed it and held it where he could see it. "I will call security and the cops."

He released me, and I exhaled, relief rushing into my limbs. Then, in a flash, he slapped the phone from my hand, and it flew several feet away. Terror filled me but was quickly replaced by rage. I pushed him. "Go. Get out of here!"

He was knocked off balance and stumbled back a few feet. I came at him, shoving him more. He laughed. "Relax, B.J. I only came to see how things were going with Nick Adams. You do quick work. Seducing him on the roof."

Had he been following us?

"Were you able to get any useful information yet? Steal any papers?"

"I told you," I hissed, "I have no intention of helping you get ammo on Nick. Now get the hell out of my condo."

"Tsk, tsk, tsk," he chided. "That kind of language shouldn't be used by a lady." He narrowed his gaze. "Or an employee."

"Ya know what?" I screamed, adrenaline raising my volume. "I'm tired of your veiled threats."

"Let me make myself clear then," he stated cooly. "You either provide me with the information I'm asking for, or you no longer work for Zonderbond and Associates."

I got closer to him, not wanting him to miss my next statement. "Well, consider this my resignation then."

He blinked, his eyes widening. "You'd quit? You don't have feelings for the S.O.B., have you? Because I can assure you, he doesn't return them. Nick Adams cares for one thing and one thing only. Himself."

I tried to keep my face neutral, not wanting him to see he'd scored a point. "It makes no difference to me. Even if you'd asked me to spy on the devil himself, I wouldn't do it for you."

He grabbed my wrist, squeezing it painfully. "You are making a mistake, B.J. I will make sure that no one in this city hires you."

I blinked away tears of frustration and anger. I knew he was right. It wouldn't even take him much effort to ruin my career. "I don't give a damn. Get. Out."

His eyes lit up. "You stupid bitch. Don't even bother to come for your property. I will have it sent to you. You have no idea what you've done in making an enemy of me. I'm a very dangerous man when I'm crossed, and I will make certain to hurt you where it hurts most." He dug his fingers into my skin before releasing me and turning to leave.

I stood, trembling, for minutes after he left, rubbing my wrist.

What have I done?

CHAPTER TWELVE

N*ick*

As the elevator doors began to shut, I went to pocket my phone and realized my wallet was missing, too. I lunged to keep the door from closing, startling the couples behind me. "Sorry," I said. "I forgot something."

I slipped into the hall and went to B.J.'s door. I raised my hand to knock and was surprised to hear a male voice inside. Curious, I leaned in.

"I came to see how things were going with Nick Adams. You do quick work. Seducing him on the roof."

What the fuck?

"Were you able to get any useful information yet? Steal any papers?"

I drew back like the door had suddenly become blazing hot.

It's all a fucking act.

I spun, and not wanting to see anyone, marched over and yanked open the door to the stairs. Once the door closed, I had to stop to take a breath, because it felt like the Denver altitude— which I'd long become accustomed to—had socked me in the gut.

She doesn't care about me. It was all an act. When will I ever learn? The only person I can count on is myself.

I debated on confronting her. But I knew I was a weak man. If she told me I'd misheard, or explain it away somehow, I might believe her.

It was all made crystal clear though when the valets pulled my car up, I got behind the wheel, and Greg Zonderbond exited her building. There could be no doubt.

I pretended it didn't matter. I'd merely had a couple of dates with the girl. It wasn't like we'd been in a relationship for months, like Zoe and I had been.

Why does it seem to hurt more than when Zoe chose Zack then?

I tried to think it through.

It has to be the betrayal. Zoe never pretended to be anything she wasn't.

And it's fresh. Tomorrow I'll feel better.

But when tomorrow came, after a night of crappy sleep, I didn't feel any better. When she texted me at eight to let me know she had my wallet, offering to bring it to me, I ignored it. She texted twice more, each time like a stab to the heart. I attempted to go about my day like my insides hadn't been ripped out and trampled on. At three when she texted, I blocked her number.

CHAPTER THIRTEEN

B.J.

When Nick didn't respond to my texts, I worried.

Maybe something's happened to him?

I talked myself off the ledge, deciding that if I hadn't heard from him by five, I'd worry then. But at four-thirty, I called his office.

"Hi. Is Nick Adams in?"

"No, he's not. Would you like to leave a message?"

Panic set in. "But he did show for work, right?"

They hesitated. "May I ask whom I'm speaking to?"

"This is B.J. McCaffrey. I—" I almost told him I had a date with Nick but then decided that I couldn't be sure that Nick would want that to be public knowledge. I cleared my throat. "Excuse me. I was trying to reach him regarding a case, and he hasn't returned my calls. I just want to make sure that he's all right."

I could practically hear his thoughts. *B.J. McCaffrey is concerned about Nick? Has hell frozen over?* But after a pause, he told me that Nick was fine. He'd been in earlier and had left for the day.

Huh.

So, he was fine. That was good... Maybe his phone wasn't working? Sure that he'd show at Bezel, I sat and waited for him for an hour plus, sipping wine and tapping my foot. I felt like an idiot.

He stood me up.

I ordered dinner but couldn't eat it. I had it boxed. I opened Nick's wallet, which I had brought with me, intending to give it to him when he got there. Seeing his address on his driver's license, I headed his way at a quick clip. It was a decent distance, but I hoped that it would cool me off. It didn't. By the time I got to Nick's, I'd worked myself into a lather. I knocked on his door so hard, I thought I'd probably bruised my knuckles. I'd thought of all the things I wanted to say to him on the walk over, but when he opened the door, I simply shoved the wallet into his hands.

"Here's your stupid wallet, you big jerk." To my horror, tears pressed on my eyelids.

"Me?" he said, acting incredulous. "At least I never lied to you."

I was taken aback. "Lied? What are you talking about?"

"Unbelievable. I'm done with this." He turned to storm into his condo, but when he went to slam the door, I grabbed it and the doorframe, bracing myself so he couldn't close it.

"Nuh-uh. You're not standing me up and—" My voice broke.

He marched away, and I stepped in. His neighbors didn't need to be witnesses to our argument. He faced me, crossing his arms. "Why don't you cut the theatrics, B.J.? Or save it for the courtroom. I know about you spying on me."

My face drained. "Spying on you? Who told you that?"

Greg?

I saw the pain he'd been trying to hide. "Nobody had to tell me." He spun his back to me again, tossing the wallet on a table. He exhaled and murmured. "I heard, okay? I heard you and Greg talking. I realize that I mean nothing to you, so you can just go now."

I moved toward him, putting a hand on him. "Oh, Nick. That's not true."

He whirled, fire in his eyes. "So, are you telling me that Greg Zonderbond wasn't at your place last night?"

"I wish he hadn't been. But he forced his way in and—"

"Come on. You expect me to believe that? Do you think I'll believe anything you say? After all the lies you've been telling me?" He snorted. "You're good, honey, but you're not that good."

I dropped my head. If he wouldn't listen to me, what was the point? I'd lost Nick, and my job in less than twenty-four hours. I slowly walked to the door. I grasped the knob to open it but first said, without turning, "You do mean something to me, Nick. And I didn't spy on you. Yes, Greg wanted me to, but I refused to play his game."

He didn't say anything, so I left, closing the door behind me.

CHAPTER FOURTEEN

Nick

In her wake, she left confusion.

Man, she was good. I could almost believe she was telling the truth.

But if I were to believe her, it would be because I wanted to believe her, not because it was the truth.

I picked the wallet up and checked its contents. Everything was there. I threw it across the room. I thought about breaking something, but I knew it wouldn't help, so I left it alone.

I was in and out of sleep all night and slept in late. The only thing that I had on my calendar was a pretrial motion hearing on one of my cases. After presenting that, I was wading through a crowd at the courthouse when I overheard the conversation in front of me between a pair of lawyers, Mike Stevenson and some guy I didn't recognize.

"Did you hear that B.J. McCaffrey left Zonderbond and Associates?"

"I know. Who would walk away from that kind of money?"

The hair rose along my neck. I followed the two until they parted at a staircase then addressed the attorney who was continuing to go my way. "Hey, Mike."

"Nick Adams." He shook my hand. "It's been a while."

"No kidding." I wasn't interested in chitchat, so I got right to the point. "Did I hear rightly that B.J. McCaffrey left Zonderbond?"

"That's right. Nuts, isn't it? And I heard Greg Zonderbond is talking her down to other firms. But I doubt she'll be on the market for long. She's too good not to get snapped up by someone."

"Yeah..." I was barely able to continue the small talk with him as my thoughts were racing.

Could she have been telling the truth?

I replayed what I'd overheard.

Yes, I heard Greg. But I never heard B.J.'s response. Why did I just assume she went along with whatever nefarious plan he had?

Isn't that what she told me at my place? Greg wanted me to, but I refused, she said.

My mind spun. She quit working with one of the top law firms in the city rather than toe the line and spy on me?

Shit. No way will she forgive me.

I plodded beside Mike mechanically.

I need to at least apologize and take whatever chewing out she gives me. I deserve it.

I called her, but of course she didn't answer. I texted her, letting her know that I believed her, but I got no response.

Just like she got no response from me last night.

I imagined her sitting at Bezel, waiting for me to show. Every minute passing, a blow to her heart. Then I thought about how she'd eventually had to slink away, embarrassed by her date standing her up. It made me sick. What an idiot I was.

I went home and made myself a frozen dinner that I didn't eat. Finally, I decided I couldn't take any more. I had to clear the air. I went to her place.

CHAPTER FIFTEEN

B.J.

As I walked home from Nick's, it felt like sacks of sugar were strapped to my legs. Being with Nick had made my life seem light for once. I wasn't consumed with my work when I was with him. And for the first time, I didn't feel so alone.

I'd kept my mind so busy with clients and cases since I'd moved to Denver that I didn't have time to think about anything else. Now I could see how empty and useless it all was. I'd clawed my way to the top to purchase a condo with a mortgage payment equal to four times the rent of the place I'd lived in when I first arrived in Denver. I'd bought blouses worth the entire wardrobe I'd brought with me from Kentucky so I could look the part I was playing. Before working at Zonderbond, I'd eaten barely enough to get by. At present I dined only at the most expensive restaurants. I had a brand-new SUV in the garage that I didn't even drive. I traded in my Suave shampoo for designer label hair products, but it couldn't erase the grime that clung to me from my impoverished youth. I may resemble a successful attorney, but nothing had truly changed. I was still the dirty little girl who deserved the beating she got from her father. No amount of schooling or prestige could wash away my worthlessness and shame.

I'd done everything in my power to erase my past and become a successful attorney. I'd worked long hours doing backbreaking, sweaty work as a welder, then I'd return to my shithole of an apartment and fall asleep on top of my law school books as I studied until my eyes burned.

And I'd thrown it all away for Nick Adams. A man I had loathed for years, despising the shallow way he treated women, his cockiness, arrogance, everything about him. Then he came unglued in the courtroom, and I let him get to me? Was I really that ignorant?

But I knew I didn't do it for Nick. It wouldn't have mattered who Greg asked me to spy on; I'd come too far to sell my soul and give up my honor in addition to everything else I'd sacrificed to get where I was. Now, within hours, I'd come to realize that I'd accomplished more than I ever dreamed of, and all I had was a deep emptiness inside and fancy baubles that couldn't satisfy the hunger that consumed me. What I'd been missing as the starving child of an alcoholic, coal-mining father wasn't objects, it was love and a sense of worth.

What do I do next?

I hadn't been foolish enough not to save for a predicament like this. I had enough banked to keep me afloat for six months. I didn't have sufficient experience to start my own firm in a place like Denver, but surely I could find a position somewhere in that amount of time, even if I had to move somewhere beyond Greg Zonderbond's reach.

I spent the next day updating my resume and studying law firms to target for employment. I made a few calls, but no one seemed to want to talk to me. Greg had gotten to them already. Throughout the morning and afternoon, I kept getting lost in thoughts about Nick. I wondered...if I gave him enough time to cool down, would he let me explain myself?

At seven, my growling stomach reminded me that I hadn't eaten all day, and I decided to get some fresh air and eat at the Chinese place around the block. When I got back to my condo and flipped the switch for my lights, nothing came on.

Great. A blackout. Could things get any worse?

Wait...

I was so tired and discouraged, I wasn't thinking properly. The lights had been on in the hall. The elevator had operated as usual. It wasn't a lack of power; I must have blown a fuse somehow.

But I wasn't even home. Did one of my appliances short the whole circuit?

He must have made a noise because I saw his silhouette in the light that filtered in from outside. Instinct had me running for the door, and I got into the hall, but he overtook me and dragged me back into the condo. I screamed for help. For someone to call the police. He told me to shut up, and when I didn't, punched me. But he made the mistake of throwing me across the room where my purse was. I retrieved my gun, staggered to my feet, aimed, and fired.

There goes my security deposit.

"What the fuck? You shot me in the leg."

I spit blood out so I could speak. "I barely nicked you. And if I have to do it again, I'll aim at a more vital area." I was breathing heavily, but my hands were surprisingly steady. "You picked the wrong Southern belle to mess with."

CHAPTER SIXTEEN

N*ick*

As I approached her neighborhood, I thought I smelled smoke. It turned out that I couldn't even get near her place. The street was blocked off and firetrucks, police cars, and ambulances huddled in front of The Randolph. As soon as I stepped from the car, I knew this wasn't any false alarm situation. The choking odor, and the ash floating in the air made that pretty clear. My heart rate kicked up a notch, and I ran. As I came around the corner, flames were licking the sides of the building and even though it was dark, I could distinguish the billows of smoke. The area of the building under attack by the fire was approximately three quarters of the way from the bottom, which was in the general area where I believed B.J.'s place to be. I ran to the barrier and tried to skirt it, but a policeman was there.

"Hey, hey, hey! Get back. Whatever you're after inside, it is not worth dying for."

"No. You don't understand." I looked skyward as if I thought that B.J.'s body might be hurtling down from above. "I think that's B.J.'s apartment." Of course, the guy had no idea what I was talking about as I had pretty much become a blathering idiot. "She's in there. I mean, I think she is. You have to—"

"Listen. I realize that you're upset, and you know someone in the building, but let's allow the pros to do their work. Your friend is probably in the crowd. Try calling him."

"Her," I said forlornly, staring at the building. "Her." I tried again. "I need to—" Then, over his shoulder, I saw someone being wheeled out on a stretcher. My stomach dropped. "Oh, my God."

The police officer twisted to see what I was commenting on, and I ducked under the sawhorse wall they'd erected and ran. I'm not sure why the policeman didn't follow me. If he was tired...? If the EMTs waved him off...?

Please, don't be B.J. Please.

The picture became clearer with each step forward. It was a woman on the stretcher. She had dark hair. It was B.J. She was motionless, her face was swollen, and I could see blood on the sheet behind her head. They kept moving, and I shuffled along with them.

"What the hell? Did you drop her?"

They gaped at me. "No, we didn't drop her," one answered indignantly. "We found her like this."

They found her like that?

"Will she be okay?"

"I'm not a doctor, but I don't think her injuries are life threatening."

"Thank God."

They'd reached the ambulance and lifted her. I stared as they began administering to her.

"Scoot back," a shorter EMT said.

Realizing he was closing the bay doors, I got out of the way. I continued to peer in the little windows. They had put an oxygen mask on her face and were assessing her head.

It dawned on me that the short EMT was gone, on his way to the front of the vehicle. I moved in that direction.

"Where are you taking her?" I shouted.

"Denver Health," he said over his shoulder, climbing into his seat.

I checked B.J. one more time, but my view was blocked by an EMT who was standing now. Without putting conscious thought into it, I walked toward where I had parked and then jogged. B.J.'s battered face kept swimming before my eyes. Had she fallen? But it appeared the injuries were both on her face and the rear of her head. How does that happen? And how did the fire start?

What the hell is going on?

Denver Health was about a mile away, so I was there in minutes. It took me longer to get to my car than to drive there. When I entered, I rushed to the closest, big, round desk. "Can you tell me where B.J. McCaffrey is?"

"Nick," a voiced rasped. A bout of coughing followed.

She was in the hall, on a gurney with the back lifted, facing the opposite direction.

"B.J." I ran over to her. "What the hell are you doing out here? Haven't they looked at you yet? I'm gonna tear someone a new one."

She grabbed my arm before I could leave. "No." She coughed some more. "They've got more important cases to handle."

"More important cases? What could be more important?"

She smiled. "The guy that was shot three times. And the guy who shot him, that the cops shot."

"Oh," I grumbled, still displeased by her being stuck in the hall and abandoned.

"How did you know I was here?"

"I saw them put you into the ambulance and asked the driver."

Her brow furrowed. "But...what were you doing there?" She coughed again and made a noise like it hurt.

"Do you want me to get you some water?"

"That would be great."

I rushed off to get a cup from a nurse and fill it at the drinking fountain.

She gulped it down. "Oh, that feels so good. Thank you."

"What the hell happened to you?"

"Well." She seemed to consider it. "They told me someone set my place on fire. They say it's arson."

"Wow. What about your face? If they dropped you, we're suing their asses."

She felt her face and winced. "Oh. Does it look bad?"

"Well, it doesn't look great," I said bluntly.

"Oh...uhh..." She seemed nervous all of a sudden.

"Not that you don't look great, because you do." I took her hand. "B.J., I'm so sorry for not believing you. That's why I came to your place. To apologize. And then it was on fire, and they were wheeling you out..."

She was staring at her sheet. "Someone was there, in my condo. I don't have any idea how they got in."

What is she talking about?

"You mean, before the fire?"

She nodded. Her face was scrunched as if she was concentrating. "I shot him."

My eyes widened. "You shot somebody?"

"Well, after he dragged me in from the hall and punched me a couple of times," she said defensively.

"Oh, I'm not questioning that he deserved it. He deserves a whole lot more, and I'd like to give it to him. Who was he?"

"I'm not sure." She was quiet for a moment. "I flipped the switch, but the lights didn't come on. He must have been watching me or how else would he know when to break in and tamper with the lights?"

"Why did he punch you? What did he want?"

"I wish I knew. The only conversation we had was him telling me to stop screaming, and then his screaming about me shooting him."

I had to chuckle. "Where did you get him?"

"In the leg, I think."

"You think? Didn't the cops get him?"

She shook her head. "Not that I know of. They haven't talked to me yet."

"Well, as a lawyer I advise you to—"

She put a hand on my chest. "Umm...I'm a lawyer too?"

"Oh, yeah."

She swatted me lightly. "You goofball."

We were quiet. "Do you need some more water?"

"Not right now. I don't want you to leave." She looked me fully in the face for the first time, and I could see that she was a little freaked out by everything. Who wouldn't be? Some guy in your house...

I brushed her hair back, being careful not to put any pressure on her bruises. "I'm sorry, B.J. I was such an asshole to you."

"That doesn't matter. It's all in the past. I'm just glad you're here." But she was staring at her sheets again.

"It does matter," I said softly. "I should have never doubted you."

"Well, I'm sure seeing Greg at my place..."

We were both silent.

"Why would some guy hit you?"

"I think he was mad that I was screaming."

"What happened after you shot him?"

She concentrated. "I don't remember. I remember me saying, you picked the wrong Southern belle to mess with."

I laughed.

"And I threatened to shoot him in other vital parts."

"Good for you."

"And then...I can't remember." She rubbed her temple. "It's like it all just fades to black there. I can't remember anything else until I woke up in the ambulance."

"B.J. McCaffrey?"

We hadn't noticed, but a young man was standing at her feet.

"Yes? That's me."

He took hold of the gurney. "I'm here to take you for a CT scan."

"Can he come?" B.J. asked quickly, grabbing my arm.

The guy gave me a once-over. "Your friend can wait here for you." He smiled down at B.J. "Are you ready to go?"

She glanced at me. "Yeah," but her voice wavered.

"I'll be right here when they bring you back. Don't worry."

The guy looked at me. "If they put her in a room, I'll come get you."

"Thanks." I squeezed B.J.'s hand, and he rolled her away. I watched until they rounded a corner.

Man, I wish I could talk to the cops. I have so many questions.

Was this random? Or was B.J. targeted? If so, why?

Could it be a client? That would be easy to believe if she were a prosecutor. But as a divorce attorney, emotions sometimes ran high, and if some nut thought she was to blame for his not getting to see his kids... Could her deadbeat dad have shown up?

Nah. She would have known it was him.

I kept going over what little I knew. He waited for her. He jumped her. Hit her. She shot him. And she doesn't remember beyond that. The head wound... The head wound didn't make sense, unless she hit it on something when he was knocking her around...

Why didn't I ask her more questions before that bozo came and took her away?

The CT scan seemed to take for-ev-er. I sat. I paced. I sat. I stretched. A belligerent drunk was hauled in and butted a cop right in front of me, opening a cut on the drunk's brow that gushed like a fire hydrant. The cop seemed no worse for wear. By two a.m., I'd shut my eyes, but the guy who'd wheeled B.J. off came back.

"Sir?"

I jumped. "Yeah. Oh, shit. Where is she?"

"They put her in a room. I can take you to her, if you want."

I chatted with Hal, which was the orderly's name, on the way to her room. He was not as big of an a-hole as I originally thought he was. He commented that the guy seemed to rough her up pretty good, but the head wound didn't seem too bad, in his uneducated opinion.

"She's right in there," he said, sweeping his arm out.

"Thanks."

He continued down the hall, and I drew a big breath before pushing through the door. I was surprised to find her alone and asleep. I crept to her bedside and stood there for a moment, gripping the rail. I sighed, running my hand along her hair.

"What a day, huh, beautiful?"

A nurse came in, and I secured my post in a chair by the window.

But one word that we had glossed over earlier kept coming back to me. Arson. She was out cold, and they set a fire around her. They were trying to kill her.

Why?

CHAPTER SEVENTEEN

Nick

I must have nodded off, because when I opened my eyes, she was awake. I scrambled to my feet. "Hey. How are you feeling?"

"Pretty good."

"Any headache?"

"No, but the cut back there burns."

"Do you think that's normal?"

She shrugged.

I brushed my palm over her matted locks. "How did you get that cut?"

She frowned. "I'm not sure."

"Did you hit your head on something? The table?"

"Not that I remember."

"Hmm."

"What time is it?"

I brought out my phone. "Three-fifteen."

"In the morning? You need to leave, Nick. Go home and get some sleep."

I hesitated.

"I'll only be sleeping anyway. You can come back tomorrow, if you want."

I bent to kiss her, trying to avoid a cut on her lip. "I want," I said meaningfully. Despite her weakened state, a charge of electricity passed through us.

A nurse chose that moment to come in, and I moved away. "How are you feeling, Ms. McCaffrey?"

"Uhh...not bad."

The nurse checked her IV and took her pulse then peered at me. "You look like hell." She winked at B.J.

"Gee, thanks," I said sarcastically, scowling at her. I shifted my gaze to B.J., who was chuckling.

"Your hair is standing up. A little bit."

I patted it down.

The nurse poured a glass of water as she asked B.J. her full name and birthdate. "Time for your Tylenol, and then you need to get some more sleep. Sleep is the great healer."

That seemed to be a cue; I eyed the nurse as I answered. "Okay. I'm taking off now." I addressed B.J. "I'll be back bright and early in the morning."

"And by bright and early, you mean after nine a.m.?" the nurse chirped.

I stared at her.

She raised her brows.

"I will be here at nine o'clock on the dot."

She nodded with a smile.

Ignoring her, I bent to give B.J. a kiss. "Get some sleep," I said quietly.

"I will."

When I got there promptly at nine, I had to wait, as the police were talking to B.J. They left, and I slipped in. B.J. seemed upset. Oddly, on her table was her partially melted welding helmet.

"Hey. What's wrong?"

"Oh, Nick." She seemed to gather herself. "How are you?"

"The question here is how are *you*?" I countered.

She exhaled. "Much better."

"Uh-huh," I answered doubtfully. "Remember, I'm a lawyer? How about the truth this time?"

"I'm doing well, physically. The doctor said I might be discharged by this evening. The CT scan showed no real fluid buildup or bleeding on the brain."

"Great," I said slowly. "Now what's the matter?"

She sighed. "Oh, it's...the police were here, and they told me my place is a total loss. The only thing the firemen salvaged was my welding hood." She peered at it. "And it's half melted."

I took her hand. "It's okay. Insurance will cover it."

"Yeah. True. But it'll be at least three months before it'll be livable." She paused, looking toward the window as if she could see her condo out there. "It's no big deal, I guess. It just came at a bad time."

"Because you quit your job?" I said gently.

Her gaze flew to me. "How...how did you know?"

"You're the talk of the courthouse, baby," I teased.

"Oh, good Lord. Don't people have anything better to talk about?"

I didn't comment.

"They're probably discussing my condo fire today, too."

"Yep." I grinned at her.

"Why are you so happy?"

I lifted her hand to kiss it. "I'm just glad you're okay."

"You're right. I'll find some way to solve my problems."

"I've got the answer for you."

She raised her brows. "You do, do you?"

"Yeah. Come stay with me while they're working on it."

She studied me and chuckled. "Yeah. Right."

"I'm serious."

"What?" She stared at me for a moment. "It's sweet of you to offer, but..."

"What? It's the logical solution."

"Nick." She shook her head. "We're not ready to live together. We've only gone out twice."

"Oh, it wouldn't be living together."

"It wouldn't."

"Nope." I didn't elaborate.

"What would it be then?"

"You'd be staying over."

"Staying over?"

"Yeah."

"For three months?"

"There'd be no strings attached. No pressure to have sex. You can—"

"Come on. We would have already done it if it weren't for a pack of teenagers."

I sucked in a breath. "Don't remind me."

She exhaled. "Are you serious?"

"I'm serious."

"I can't do that."

"Sure, you can."

"I don't think it's a good idea."

Eventually she caved, and we became housemates. She moved in with the pair of jeans she had on when she was attacked, a Denver Health T-shirt (as the blouse she had on was torn and had blood on it), and her half-melted welding helmet.

CHAPTER EIGHTEEN

B.J.

It was three days after I was released from the hospital. I was wearing a new maroon suit with a matching scarf and toting a new briefcase that held only the resume I'd downloaded from the cloud onto Nick's computer and a pad of legal paper with a pen. I had to do so many things, including getting a new driver's license and credit cards, things one didn't typically think about having lost in a fire.

Where I usually didn't wear much makeup, I had it caked on today, trying to hide the bruises and cuts. I wanted to spend the interview I was headed for discussing my litigation skills not my messed-up face. I had to force myself to not stare at my burned condo as I climbed the courthouse steps. I needed to stay focused. I needed this job.

I took it as a good omen when I saw Nick in the crowded atrium. He had his back to me and was joking around with a bunch of guys as I approached.

"So, Nick," one said, shooting a look at his pal, "I heard that the B.J. in B.J. McCaffrey stands for blow job because she's so good on her knees. Is that true?"

I gaped, feeling like I'd been splashed with ice water.

Nick was laughing. "Well..."

I didn't want to hear his answer. I walked away at a fast clip, but I heard someone call Nick's name in a warning tone, and I heard his "oh, shit!"

"B.J., wait."

The group of guys roared.

Pretty funny calling someone a vile name like that.

My face was flaming hot, and I forced tears back, picking up my pace as I heard Nick getting closer. My stomach rolling, I ducked behind a wall and pressed against the cool marble, putting a hand on my stomach.

"B.J." Nick said, rounding the corner and breathing heavily.

My embarrassment turned to anger in a flash. "Don't you call me that. Don't you ever call me that. I don't want to hear that coming out of your mouth again."

His brow furrowed. "O-okay," he said tentatively. "What am I supposed to call you then? Barbara Jean?"

"No. That name is only for my tax returns and diplomas," I snapped.

"Well, then what?" he huffed.

I searched my mind. "Bobby Jo."

"Bobby Jo?"

He was getting on my last, frayed nerve. "Yeah. Bobby Jo. What's wrong with Bobby Jo?"

He waved his hands. "Nothing. Nothing. I just...I've never heard you called that."

"That's what my daddy called me."

"Okay."

"I have to go. I have an interview."

"Shit," he said, rubbing his chin, not looking at me at first. Then he lifted his gaze. "B.J." He closed his eyes. "Scratch that. Bobby Jo, I'm so sorry you heard that."

"Yeah, I bet you are," I spat. I tried to storm past him, but he grabbed me.

"Please. I would never mean to hurt you."

"Well, you did, Nick." I swallowed a sob. "If you cared for me, you'd want to go to war with anyone who talked about me that way."

"I-I know. I was wrong. I was gonna shut him down. I was. But I should have done it sooner."

I was seething. I took in a ragged breath. "Well, it's too bad for you, Nick, because I don't give guys second chances." I was so angry, my head hurt. I ripped my arm out of his grasp and marched away.

Needless to say, it wasn't the best interview I'd ever had. But I made it through it. Luckily, I guess, I didn't have much to pack when I got back to Nick's place. I put most of what I did have into my briefcase, snagged my welding hood, and attempted to flag a taxi. While my SUV wasn't damaged in the fire, my key had been melted, and I hadn't had the chance to get a new one from the dealer. When three straight taxis ignored me, my shout of frustration drew some unwanted attention. Then I walked the mile to the bus station in my high heels. My phone was another casualty of the fire, so I couldn't Uber. I dropped by the shelter, which was a block away from the bus station, and said my good-byes to the animals.

I exhaled when I got into my seat on the bus and stared out the window. I hadn't cried. I wouldn't cry.

It's better to not feel.

Even with the thirty-hour drive to Harlan, I hesitated to get off the bus when we got there.

"Ma'am? Ain't this your stop?"

I breathed deeply. "Yes, Redd, it is." Thirty hours gave me time to get to know the driver. I pulled myself up on the chair in front of me.

When I got to the front, Redd addressed me. "Good luck now, Miss Bobby Jo."

"Thank you, Redd. I hope your wife is back on her feet soon."

"Thank ya."

The house hadn't changed one iota. Maybe the gray siding—which was actually white siding, covered in coal dust—was slightly more cracked. The screen door maybe hung a bit more crookedly, but the changes were negligible. I climbed the rickety steps. The front door was open, letting in the breeze through the screen. He was slumped in a rocking chair, half in sunlight, half in shadow. He'd sat in the chair so often, they had a semi-symbiotic relationship; his body's imprint was worn into the wood of the rocker, and at the same time, his back seemed to have morphed into the shape of the chair.

"Well, if it ain't ol' Bobby Jo McCaffrey."

"Hi, Daddy. Can I come in?"

"I guess you can do what ya want," he drawled.

I gingerly opened the door and stepped into the room, leaning my briefcase against the wall and placing my hood by it.

He sat up. An empty fifth was at his feet, one that was three-fourths gone rested on the side table near him. "What the hell are you doin' here?"

I cleared my throat. "I-I've come to start a business in town. I thought you'd want to be informed."

"What happened? You get your ass fired from that fancy law firm ya worked at? Cuz ya sure didn't come here of your own design, seeing as ya ain't been back here since ya left."

I lowered my gaze. "That's a legitimate charge, Daddy. I'm sorry."

"You're sorry all right," he said meanly, spitting on the floor. "That's for damn sure."

I wouldn't let him tear me down. "The road goes both ways, Daddy. You could have come to see me."

"We both know who can afford a tank of gas, and who can't."

I felt the tears forming and blinked them away. What he'd said hit home, but I wouldn't let him see it. "That's true. It's my fault. I'm sorry." I inhaled. "Well, I just came to tell you..."

"Wait a second." He unfolded himself from his rocker. He came over and grabbed my chin, and I fought not to flinch. He rotated my head back and forth. His eyes widened. "Someone been whoopin' on you, gal? Is that why ya came home?"

"No."

He studied me, working his jaw. "But someone's been whoopin' on ya. That's for sure." He turned to hobble to his chair with a limp that wasn't there when I left home. "Or maybe it's 'cuz your lux'ry apartment burned down."

I couldn't have been more surprised. "How—how did you hear about that?"

He shrugged. "I watch the news."

My brow wrinkled. "The *Denver* news?"

He rolled a shoulder. "May've come up in my social media feed."

I scanned the room briefly. *Does he actually own a computer now or is he bullshitting me? How does he even know where I live? Err...lived.* I'd never had any visitors from Harlan, that I could recall, that could have brought the information back with them. I would have asked further if I hadn't been wanting to get away as soon as possible.

"It may have had something to do with the fire at The Randolph, but it doesn't matter. I'm here, and I'm opening my own business."

He sneered. "Good for you." The words were laced with venom.

It shook me. "I didn't come to brag; I just wanted you to know so you wouldn't be surprised to see me in town or hear about my business. I'll go now so you can continue the busy work that you've been doing here." I couldn't help the jab. I was sick of him making me feel worthless. I whirled and bolted outside, slamming the rattletrap screen door. I made it down the steps onto the dirt path that led to them. I put a hand to my temple, unsure if the headache that felt like I'd been pierced by a welding rod was due to my recent concussion or the ancient pain inflicted by my father. Ignoring the footpath, I hoofed it across his patchy lawn to the road.

I hadn't even gotten a few yards when I heard the screen door close behind me. I knew he was on the porch watching me, but I didn't turn. He coughed, and I tried to ignore the fact that the hacking sounded far worse than when I'd left, but it still lodged somewhere in the back of my mind.

By the time I got to the Rodeway Inn—the name irked me as it should have been Roadway Inn with an A not an E—I was sweaty, grimy, and bone tired. My new suit was a mess, wrinkled from the bus ride, filthy from the walk. The inn had a kind of cute, homey logwood cabin feel to it. They'd done some recent upgrades that made the rooms a bit less depressing, but the bathroom was scary. Yes, I lived in a plush place in Denver, but I'd also lived in worse places in the past, and I wasn't such a snob that I couldn't deal with it.

I stripped out of my suit to take a shower, laying clean towels over the cracked, putrid-orange tile that, coupled with the black grout in between them, had a spidery, Halloween air to it. The faucet squeaked loudly as I fought it open, and I was hit with the bracing cold water left in the shower head before the hot water reached it. I shivered, rubbing my arms as I waited for the temperature to rise, and I wasn't all that surprised when the sobs hit me. I covered my face, my shoulders shaking now from more than the chill of the water.

I had vowed never to come back here. But I wouldn't stay with a man who didn't respect me. It's why I'd left my father in the first place. Only it hurt a little more with Nick, because I'd convinced myself that he cared for me. The voices swirled around me hellishly.

"I heard that the B.J. in B.J. McCaffrey stands for blow job because she's so good on her knees. Is that true?"

"You're sorry all right. That's for damn sure."

"Why don't you cut the theatrics, B.J.? Or save it for the courtroom. I know about you spying on me."

"You are making a mistake, B.J. I will make sure that no one in this city hires you."

"At least I never lied to you."

"You stupid, bitch. Don't even bother to come for your property. I will have it sent to you. You have no idea what you've done in making an enemy of me. I'm a very dangerous man when I'm crossed, and I will make certain to hurt you where it hurts most."

But eventually, the late-arriving hot water melted the voices, sending them down the drain. I straightened my spine.

That's the last time I cry because of this.

I toweled off, changed into my Denver Health T-shirt and a new pair of underwear I'd gotten when I purchased my suit, and flopped onto the bed, not bothering to get under the sheets or blow-dry my hair. It would be a rat's nest when I woke up, but I was beyond exhausted after the shitty rest on the bus and in the hospital. But in my sleep, I was haunted by my father's wracking cough, and my anxiety over my future.

CHAPTER NINETEEN

N*ick*

I knew it the moment I got home. Her welding helmet wasn't on my coffee table, and whatever few belongings she'd had were gone. I squeezed my eyes shut, fighting the pain.

Why do you have to be such a complete asshole, Nick?

I slung my briefcase into the nearest chair and crossed to the couch, lowering myself onto it with a sigh. I messed up again. Another relationship in the toilet because I couldn't seem to love or care for anyone besides myself. I laid my head on the top of the couch and stared at the ceiling.

The logical thing to do would be to forget B.J.—Bobby Jo, and begin again.

But I'd never been one for logic.

Where could she have gone? I couldn't call her to beg for forgiveness since her cell phone had been turned to liquid in the fire. She had no friends that I knew of. I didn't know where her siblings lived, and I'm not even sure she did. She'd never go back to Harlan. I had no idea where to search for her.

I tried to concentrate on the work I'd brought home, but it was a lost cause. It struck me suddenly. Maybe she went to the dog shelter to say goodbye. I knew it was probably useless, but I hopped in the car anyway and drove there. It wasn't a big surprise when she wasn't there, but it still was a letdown. I walked Bruno and a few other dogs, did a little cleanup, and made my way toward the parking lot. I was so distracted that I almost plowed into a veterinarian technician as I left the kennel area.

"Oh, hey, Nick."

I gave her a smile, although I didn't feel smiley. "Sorry about that, Susie. How's it going?"

"Good. And you?"

"Good, thanks." Why do we ask people how they are when we all answer good when we're not? "Have a nice weekend." Did she need my permission for that?

"You, too."

I dipped my head and passed her.

"Too bad you weren't here sooner," she called.

I spun, and she was standing in the doorway. "Why's that? Did I miss something?"

"B.J. was here. You guys like to walk dogs together, don't you?"

I could hardly believe my ears. I hurried toward her. "B.J. was here?"

Taken aback by my energetic return, she answered. "Yes. A couple of hours ago."

Damn. "Did she say where she was going?"

"Uhh...no. Why?" Her suspicion turned into excitement. "Were you guys meeting for a date?"

I pinched my bottom lip. "Yeah. No. Sort of. You're sure she didn't mention any place she might be going? Did she give any indication that she would be back?"

"No, she didn't." She tilted her head. "In fact, she was unusually quiet. She seemed...sad."

It was a stab to the gut, but Susie had no way of knowing that. "Okay. Thanks."

I exited the building and blew out a breath.

She was here. If only I'd left a little earlier...

Although I knew it was useless, I went to the courthouse. Maybe she had another interview there. Of course, I didn't see her, but I ran into Rick Tonkin, the guy I'd been speaking with when B.J.—Bobby Jo, will I ever get used to that—overheard us.

"Hey, man. I'm sorry if I got you in hot water earlier."

"No. It's my fault. I should have ripped you a new one for referring to her like that."

He blinked but then laughed. "Oh, yeah. You mean if you knew she saw you. That would have been great. She would have probably gone down on you to thank you."

I stared at him, my jaw tensing. But how could I blame him when I would have done the same thing at one time?

"Oh," he said haltingly. "You're serious, aren't you?"

"Yeah, I'm serious. I'm dead serious. Don't you ever talk about B.—Bobby Jo again in that manner."

He chuckled. "Bobby Jo? That's what B.J. stands for?"

I was becoming more annoyed. "Yes. What's wrong with Bobby Jo?"

"Well, nothing, I guess, if you're a hick."

Again, I wanted to grind him into the floor. But how could I? I'd be a hypocrite. I gripped his shoulder, maybe a bit too tightly. "Listen, Rick." I took in a breath through my teeth, looking off into the distance so I could keep my cool. "I know I used to speak of women in that way. And I used to treat women poorly, too. I was an asshole. Don't be an asshole, Rick. If you can't do that, don't consider us friends anymore. I'm sorry if that disappoints you, but I'm more sorry that I hurt the feelings of the woman I love, and I don't want to ever do that again, to anyone." I patted him then grasped him again roughly. I wanted to make sure he understood I was serious. "Got it?"

"Yeah, sure, Nick."

"Good." I began to move past him and froze in my tracks when I heard his parting remark.

"If you're okay with being pussy-whipped, I can't stop you."

I closed my eyes and slowly spun on my heel. "What did you say?"

He stuck his chest out. "I think you heard me."

Dude, you're an idiot for taking me on right now. I'd like nothing more than to turn my self-loathing on your ass. But somehow, I don't think that's the high road.

And if I was taking the high road, then it would be my only avenue of travel from here on.

Walk away, Nick. Just walk away.

The resistance to not club the guy made my legs feel like they were screws too big for their holes; it required extra effort to move them.

"Yeah, that's what I thought," he taunted.

Keep walking.

Rick yelled some more things after me, but I ignored him, surprised by how much like an idiot he sounded. I decided I liked the high road. Less bruised knuckles, less regrets.

However, I still had my remorse over how I'd initially reacted to the situation. And the fallout was hell. I crossed the street to The Randolph and meandered around the lobby a little in a futile effort to find her. I considered entering Unwarranted but found the high road didn't go there.

I exited via the front door and searched the sidewalk in both directions. I caught the obnoxious Zonderbond and Associates sign down the block from the courthouse. Maybe they'd know something that could help me. It felt weird being in enemy territory. The first thing I noticed was the blonde behind the desk doing her nails. She seemed familiar, but I couldn't place her. I ambled in, keeping my eye open for Greg. I turned on the charm.

"Hi there. Is Greg Zonderbond in?" Best to be aware if he was around.

"No. Can I help you?"

"Uhh...maybe. Wow." I stared at her nails, painted like an American flag. "Those are so cool. Did you do that yourself?"

Her smile grew wider. "Yeah. I did."

"That's amazing. How do you make those tiny stars?"

"It's hard."

"I bet it is. Say, is Bobby Jo McCaffrey in?"

How about that? I got it right.

"I think it's Barbara Jean, and she's no longer with the firm." She narrowed her gaze on me. "What did you say your name was?"

"I didn't say." I looked at her nameplate. "I see yours is Michelle. Very pretty. Would you have any idea where Ms. McCaffrey might be?"

"I have no clue."

Darling, you have no idea how true that statement is. "Huh. There was a fire at her condo, and it's currently uninhabitable. Has she ever mentioned staying at any friends' or acquaintances' houses?"

"Nah. B.J.'s a loner. She's all business, all the time."

Except when she's with me.

"Why are you asking about her? Are you a cop?"

"No, no. Just a friend. Has she ever mentioned wanting to live anywhere besides Denver?"

"Look, I'm afraid I can't help you. B.J. kept to herself. I have no idea where she may be."

I might as well leave. Clearly, she's of no help to me.

"Huh." I stared at her a moment, having finally placed her. "Have a nice night." I spun and headed to the door. She was the blonde who had seduced my client, Alvis Mahafey.

I'm sure Greg put her up to it. He wanted to embarrass me. That son of a bitch.

I whirled back around, making her jump. "Where is Greg?"

"I'm afraid he's at the hospital with his wife."

I took an involuntary step forward. "Sarah? Sarah's sick?"

"You know Sarah?"

"Yes, we all went to law school together."

"I see. Well, she— Wait a minute. The sole person he's mentioned from law school is Nick Adams. You're not Nick Adams, are you?"

I grinned. *The one and only.*

"Thanks again for your help, Michelle. Have a good night." With that, I left.

Sarah's sick. No wonder Greg's acting so erratically.

It pained me to hear it. Sarah was a nice woman.

Once on the street, I couldn't help but look at Bobby Jo's building. Either the arsonist didn't understand what he was doing, or the fire people did one hell of a job, because I'd heard Bobby Jo's and two other apartments had been damaged, but no others. I thought about our night on the roof.

I trudged to the car and drove home. As soon as I entered, the room felt way too empty without her. I cracked a beer, sat on the couch, and put the game on the TV, but I couldn't concentrate on it. I glanced down at the couch. Beside me was the blanket I'd used the night before when I'd slept there and she in my bed. I rose and wandered to my bedroom, switching on the light. I leaned against the doorframe and took a long pull on my beer. She'd made the bed. It made me smile. Then I saw a small notecard propped against the pillows. I set my beer on the highboy dresser and crossed to snatch up the paper.

THANKS FOR BEING A GENTLEMAN AND GIVING ME THE BED.

And she'd drawn a winky face.

SERIOUSLY, I REALLY APPRECIATE YOUR KINDNESS IN TAKING ME IN.

That was followed by a heart and her initials. Clearly, she'd written it prior to me trampling her feelings to dust.

"Damn," I murmured.

I'm sorry, B.J.—shit, will I ever stop calling her that?—Bobby Jo.

I strode to the highboy, and rested my arms on it, rereading what she'd wrote and flash carding through our memories together while I finished my beer. I decided that the day needed to end and leisurely went around locking doors, brushing my teeth, preparing for bed.

Maybe if I got some sleep, I'd find a solution to everything in the morning. Little did I know, the day had no intention of ending. I tossed and turned in my bed, finally getting up to sleep on the couch. I thought about how strange it was that I hadn't thought of Zoe all day. Eventually, I fell asleep.

My phone rang. I entertained a fleeting fancy that it was her, but Clint McGuire's name glowed on the screen, along with the time, quarter to three.

I rolled onto my back and answered. "Clint?"

Clint got straight to the point. "I got a notification from the firm's Ring camera. Someone broke into our office. I called the police and am heading down there."

I sat up. "What?"

"Oh..."

"Oh, what?"

"I'm looking at the video. Wow...I think you need to see this. I'm sending it over." The line clicked off. I waited about five minutes, and the phone glowed again. I pushed play on the video he'd sent. While I was still viewing it, he called.

"Did you get the video?"

"Yeah, I'm watching it."

"It's her, Nick. It's B.J."

It did resemble her. The red suit, dark hair, white cowboy hat. She'd been lying all along. She broke into our office, probably to get at files.

"I'll be right behind you."

When I got there, Clint and two police officers were in a little huddle in the middle of the room. "Here he is. This is Nick Adams, the head of the firm."

"Hiya." I shook hands with the policemen as they introduced themselves. They turned to Clint. "So, you said you have some Ring video."

"Yeah. Show 'em, Nick."

I was holding my phone, but I hesitated.

Clint looked at me. "Show them, Nick," he said more forcefully.

I played the video for them.

"And you say you recognize this woman?"

Since I didn't answer, Clint did. "Yes, that's B.J. McCaffrey. She works for a rival firm."

They directed their attention to me. "Would you agree with that, sir?"

I shifted my weight from one foot to another. Clint glared at me so hard his eyes were bulging. "The picture isn't that great..."

Clint threw his arm out to indicate me. "Permission to treat the witness as hostile."

We all stared at him.

"We're not in court, Clint."

"I know we're not in court," he grumbled and turned fully to the policemen. "Nick was seeing B.J."

"Is that true, sir?"

I slid my jaw back and forth. "We did see each other a time or two."

"Do you believe this B.J. McCaffrey is the woman in the video?"

I couldn't deny it. The evidence was in my hand. She'd betrayed me. She'd betrayed us all.

I exhaled, dropping my head. "Yes, it's her."

"All right then. We'll pick her up and bring her in for questioning."

I scratched my neck. "About that..."

"Yes?"

"She's sort of missing."

"Missing?"

"Yes. She's gone, and I have no idea where she is."

"Oh, come on!" Clint cried out in exasperation.

"It's true."

They questioned me some more, and finally we all left. I stumbled home hoping to get at least a few hours' sleep. At seven a.m. sharp, my phone rang. Clint. He must have decided that seven o'clock was a decent enough hour to call.

"Have you seen the news?"

I grabbed the remote and turned the TV on, swinging my legs to the floor and standing. "The Nuggets lost in overtime?"

"Not the Nuggets, you..." He must have decided, since I was his boss, to eat the expletive. "Channel Six. Look at Channel Six."

"And movie star Johnny Caine is in hot water again. Literally," the voice said as video played behind her of the celebrity going at it with a woman in a hot tub who was clearly not his wife. "But that's not even the most damning video," the anchorwoman stated.

This was a disaster. "Oh, shit."

They played video of Johnny Caine walking around his very pregnant wife's prone form, berating and kicking her.

I groaned, closing my eyes. "This isn't good."

"No shit!" Clint snapped. "You better find that girlfriend of yours because she's going to jail." He disconnected. A riled-up Clint wasn't a pleasant thing to deal with.

I sank back down onto the couch. "Oh, B.J. What have you done?" Even though she'd been using me, I still didn't want to see her go to jail. I searched for my phone and played the Ring footage again.

I couldn't deny it looked like her. I watched it like six times, my heart dropping a little lower with each viewing.

"Wait..." I rewound to a section where the intruder had her hand on the door. My spirit soared. I popped to my feet to get dressed and headed to the police station.

CHAPTER TWENTY

B*obby Jo*

I had just spooned in a mouthful of mashed potatoes when the door creaked open, and I froze. I don't understand why it hit me so hard. I'd known that eventually we'd run into each other. When your town only had a half dozen restaurants, it was bound to happen.

He seemed a bit dazed as he walked into Huddle House, a cute little diner. He made his way to my table, and tipped his hat to me, which he'd never in my life done.

"Bobby Jo, may I sit with you?"

I almost choked on my potatoes. Daddy never, *never* asked me permission for *anything*. All I could manage was a small nod.

"So..." He sat, bent over, and spun his hat in his hand, spacing out.

I chewed, swallowed, and waited for him to speak, but he didn't. "Daddy?"

He jumped. "Huh? Oh...uhh...how's the...job goin'? Your attorneyin'?"

He was asking about my life? Was he simply baiting me to find something to ridicule me for? I cleared my throat. "Well, to be honest, it's been slow. I've...uhh...gotten some welding work. ...On the side," I added when he didn't comment.

"Uhh-huh." He bobbed his head loosely, with the same wide-eyed look on his face.

"Is something wrong?" I asked cautiously.

"Somethin' wrong? Nothin's wrong. Can't a dad have breakfast with his baby girl..."

Now I'm his baby girl? Something's definitely off.

"...without gettin' guff about it?"

"Of course." *It's just you never have.*

He slapped his hat on his knee. "Alrighty then," he said with an edge, loud enough that the group of farmers at a table across from us gave us a look.

I kept my head down and put another bite into my mouth to give me something to do.

"You staying at that Rodeside place?" His gaze darted to me and away several times.

"Uhh, yes. Yes, I am."

He again nodded. "Good. Good. That's a nice place."

"Uh-huh."

"Not like your place in Denver, mind you, but, all in all..." His words trailed off.

"Yes. It's cute. I like it there," I said truthfully.

"Yep. Yep. ...It's not too expensive there, is it?"

This was shaping up to be one of the oddest conversations of my life. "No. No." He continued to stare at me, so I added. "Only $71 a night."

"Seventy-one dollars a night, huh? That's pretty good, ain't it?"

I don't think my father had ever spent a night anywhere other than Harlan, so hotel prices were a bit out of his wheelhouse.

"Yes. Very good."

He brushed something from the table with his hat. I resisted the urge to check the floor. "Ya could stay with me. Iffin ya wanted to," he added quickly.

"Oh. That's very nice of you to offer. It's just, I thought, maybe a grown woman alone with a...family member of the opposite sex. Well, you know how people like to talk."

"Yeah. Yeah. That was smart." He stared at his hat. "Ya think they would feel the same way with a short visit, like?"

Was he asking me to visit him? "No. I think a short visit would be fine, don't you?"

"I reckon it would." He coughed, and it almost seemed like he couldn't catch his breath.

I jumped to my feet. "Daddy! Do you need some water?"

He waved me off, although he was still coughing. He held a red bandana up to his mouth. People again were sliding us glances. One of the farmers at the table of four was eyeing me with alarm, which is how I was looking at him. Finally, Daddy regained control.

"So stupid," he muttered. "I think I need to go, angel."

Angel?

"I can go with you." I reached for my purse to pay for my food.

"No, no. You stay here and finish your meal. I'll see you soon." He rose and rushed out before I even knew what was happening.

Angel?

I slowly sat, exchanging looks again with a few of the farmers at the next table. I'd completely lost my appetite. My father had been abducted by aliens. It was the only possible explanation.

CHAPTER TWENTY-ONE

N*ick*

I marched up to the detective's desk. "B.J. McCaffrey is innocent, and I can prove it."

He stared at me then spoke slowly. "That's a tad too much energy for..." He checked his watch. "...eight in the morning. I've barely had my coffee."

"Check this video." I went around to his side of the desk, perhaps a smidge too forcefully, and he retreated a little. I held out my phone. "This is the Ring footage. That appears to be B.J.'s hat and suit."

"But it's not?" he guessed.

"Just wait." I let it play until it got to the frame I wanted and froze the picture on the image of her hand on the door as she opened it. "There."

He looked from me to it and back. "I don't get it."

I exhaled and zoomed in on it. "See?"

He shook his head. "I'm afraid not."

"The fingernails."

"What about them? They're cute, but what does it have to do with the case?"

"Bobby Jo would never do that to her nails. Hers are always one uniform color, without any embellishment."

He seemed incredulous. "Mr. Adams...the color of someone's nails is not proof that—"

"What if I told you that a girl from our rival firm has her nails done exactly like this."

He grinned. "Now you're getting closer."

"And...it just dawned on me. B.J. had a hat like that, but it burned in a recent fire. She got none of her clothes out; those are gone, too. Other than the ones she was wearing. And...there are no scars. B.J. has little scars all over her hands, defensive wounds from a broken beer bottle."

"So, you're saying someone was trying to frame her."

"That's precisely what I'm saying. Barbara Jean McCaffrey did not break into our office."

"Well, I'll have to do some investigating, but it sure looks like you're right."

"So, since I solved your case for you and all, could you do me a favor and check her credit card so that I can find her?"

He smiled broadly. "You're a lawyer. You know I can't do that. You could be a stalker boyfriend."

I gasped. "Me? You think *I'm* a stalker boyfriend?"

"No. I don't think you're a stalker boyfriend, and I've got pretty good instincts..." He held up, as if considering it.

My heart did a mini leap.

But he was a tease. "But there's no way to be sure, so I'm not doing it."

I sighed. "Yeah, I didn't think so." But at least I had cleared her good name.

Months had passed, and I was sitting morosely at my desk, thinking about her. I rose and went to the window, focusing on the mountains surrounding our fair city. They were calling me. I slammed my laptop closed and left early. A rigorous hike might help me get her off my mind. So, I hiked. Actually, more climbed, taking a steep course that probably wasn't the wisest, but required all my concentration and strength to complete. I left the park sweaty, dirty, scraped a little...and still thinking of her.

I went home and showered, drank a beer—I'd switched from my fancy imported ones to a solid Anheuser-Busch product—put a game on, and continued to think of her. I picked up my laptop idly, checked a few emails, then watched the tube without really seeing it. Unconsciously, I typed her name in, stole a drink of my beer, and stared at it. Then I hit enter. I sat forward, my heart pounding, and read.

McCaffrey Metalworks, **Bobby Jo McCaffrey**, proprietor. 102 Eversole St, Harlan, KY 40831.

Underneath it was a listing for Barbara Jean McCaffrey, attorney at law, with the same address.

Leaving my beer half drunk, I climbed over the coffee table—instead of going around, for some reason—went to the bedroom, and dug out my leather duffle bag. I jammed clothes into it, full of hope for the first time in a long time.

I pulled in front of a cottage and had to keep myself from running up the steps that cut into the hill at the bottom of her front lawn. I stared at the window as I traversed the short sidewalk, hoping for a sighting, or at least a flutter of the curtains. A sign on the door read closed. I turned the knob anyway. It was locked.

Checking the area, I slid behind some bushes to peer in her window, my hand bridging my forehead and the glass. Inside the room seemed to be divided in two. One side had a counter and display cases and a sign for McCaffrey Metalworks, with a cool logo making the "M"s look like mountains. The logo was on a large piece of metal with a bronze finish. Underneath that, her slogan was painted: Art to melt your heart, fired and formed from my imagination and a little heat. On the opposing side—or opposite side, as most normal people would call it—was a sweet rolltop desk with Barbara Jean McCaffrey, attorney-at-law on a similar sign. It had another sharp logo that combined her name with the outline of a tree. On the left was the writing; on the right, half of the tree was defined by open space. Beneath it was painted: When your case needs both heart and heat.

She can definitely bring the heat in the courtroom...and other places as well.

I smiled at the thought then left the window as a car was driving by, and I didn't want anyone mistaking me for a Peeping Tom.

Now what?

I rode around town some. It had a population of a little under two thousand; surely, I could find her. But a half hour later, discouraged and hungry, I pulled in front of a business called Huddle House. Every head turned when I entered, conversation stopped, and I was given the once-over by a half-dozen pairs of eyes. Feeling a tad overdressed, even though I was wearing jeans and a lightweight sweater, I shifted my weight from side to side, searching for either a wait-for-hostess sign, or a seat-yourself sign. People took up talking again, and the waitress behind the counter said, in a friendly enough Kentucky twang, "Seat yourself, sugar."

I sat at a table near a party of four, two in overalls, two in jeans. Four hats were perched on the ledge of the back of their booth, either baseball or cowboy-style. My table hadn't been wiped, but it had been bussed and was the only two-seater open. The waitress topped off cups at the next table then addressed me. "Can I get ya some coffee?"

"Uhh...no thank you. But could I get a Pepsi?"

"We just have Coke."

"That'll be fine. Thank you."

She left, and I perused the menu, thinking the special of turkey and mashed potatoes looked outstanding. I couldn't help but hear the country-slow, deep baritone voice of the customer nearest me.

He was chuckling and saying, "And I don't envy her none. That Hal McCaffrey is a piece of work."

"Pretty young thing, though," another commented, and they mumbled or nodded agreement. "Soft on the eyes."

"Don't you let Janice catch you sayin' that. She'd skin you alive."

They all laughed and then fell silent for a moment.

"Ya seen his place lately? It'd 'bout crumble around ya if ya sneezed hard enough. He don't give its maintenance more than a lick and a promise."

They carried on for a bit, but I tuned out.

It has to be her father, or grandfather, or uncle, or some kind of relative.

I Googled McCaffrey's in town then scanned the names, stopping at Henry McCaffrey.

Could it be him?

I made note of the address, deciding that it would be my next destination. When the turkey came, it was even better than it appeared to be on the menu. I snarfed it down, skipped the cherry pie that had looked equally tempting, and left.

When I pulled in front of the address, I had little doubt I was at the right place. The house number dangled off the mailbox crookedly, swinging from one chain as the other chain was broken. An old-fashioned push mower lay in the middle of the yard that was cut about a fourth of the way some time ago, like the owner had been caught up in the rapture, leaving it discarded. I sat in the car, hand on the ignition button, second guessing myself as to whether or not I should be at this stranger's house. But I stabbed the button to kill the engine and crossed the lawn, which was both patchy, and at the same time, overgrown, taking the meandering dirt path that led to the door. The front door was open, so I banged on the screen door, jumping to hold it on when it seemed to be falling.

"Whatcha want?"

I peered through the dirty screen's gridwork and could barely discern somebody in a rocking chair in a dark room.

"Hello." I cleared my throat. "I was searching for Bobby Jo McCaffrey. Have you seen her?"

"Just who wants to know?" he replied, his voice heavy with suspicion.

I squinted, trying to make him out better to determine his age and possible connection to Bobby Jo. "I'm— Uhh...can I come in?"

He spit to the side. "Suit yourself."

"Thank you." I carefully opened the screen door, watching the hinges as I did, closing it softly. "Hi." I walked over to shake hands with the man. "I'm Nick Adams."

He wiped his palms on his dusty denims, which I wasn't at all sure was helpful, and gave me a hard shake. Despite his wiry build, he was surprisingly strong, looking older than Bobby Jo's father would have been.

"You the reason my daughter's back here?"

Oops, I guess it is her dad.

"Uhh...I'm not sure. I'd like to talk to her though. Do you know where I can find her?"

He sat and rocked, staring at me for an uncomfortably long time. "I s'pose she's at her business, up the way some, on the right." He gestured down the street. "But if ya've come to make trouble for her, I suggest ya leave," he added slowly, an edge to his tone. "Bobby Jo's had plenty of heartache in her life. She don't need any more."

The old codger was trying to intimidate me, but, strong or no, it would take more than him, and the four big guys at the table at the Huddle House, to keep me from her. "I get that. I owe her an apology though, and I'm giving it to her."

He stopped abruptly, leaning forward. "You do that then, son, and then get your happy ass on out of town. Ya hear?"

"Yeah. I hear," I grumbled. I left and considered slamming the door off its rusty hinges.

The high road, Nick. Take the high road.

CHAPTER TWENTY-TWO

B*obby Jo*

I was washing the breakfast dishes when I heard the bells jingle above the door in front. I quickly dried my hands and pushed through the swinging door that led to my businesses.

"I'm sorry to keep you waiting. I—"

I lifted my head, and Nick was standing there in dark jeans and a gray sweater, his fists jammed in his pockets, as fresh and handsome as the day was long. Definitely a stranger to Harlan. I felt like I couldn't breathe.

"Nick?" My voice rang with the pain of our separation.

"Hi, Bobby Jo," he said softly, taking a tentative step forward. "You look good."

I glanced down. I had chosen to wear a dress today, mostly because I needed to do the laundry. It was a white, halter-top-style dress that was probably more gray at this point in the day. I wanted to thank him for the compliment, but my mouth wouldn't cooperate. The words tore from my heart. "Why are you here?"

"I came to find you," he replied simply.

The scene in the courthouse of him yucking it up with his buddies at my expense came to my mind. "So, you found me," I said, fighting to keep my voice steady and sound as indifferent as possible. I was pissed as hell at the fact that I ached to touch him. An odd moment passed while we stood and stared at each other, a powerful force between us, his gaze intense with an inner fire. It was as if I was channeling through all my various reactions to seeing him and rejecting each feeling, one at a time, my brain attempting to rule over my heart.

He came all the way from Denver? Maybe he is more serious about our relationship than I thought...

How serious can he be if he let someone freakin' demean you?

Then he became reanimated, sliding to a rack housing some of my artwork. "These are amazing. Is this one available? I'd like to buy it for above my bed." He indicated a large piece with a cutout that looked like a mountain range. The mention of his bed moved me at my core. The night on the rooftop flashed in my mind. I nodded, dumbly. "And I want this one, too. I just haven't decided where to put it. Do you have any ideas?" I couldn't discuss the mundane when so much turmoil was going on inside me. I shifted my gaze from him to the work in question, and it remained transfixed. It was of a longhorn sheep ascending a steep rise, with the negative space defining its shape. A slice in the hill represented water running down the slope. I managed to shake my head a little. "Well, I'll determine what to do with it when I get it back to my place. This one..." he pointed to an item the length of a garage door and half the size, of the Denver skyline, "I want for my office, and that horse statue...I want that one, but I don't know if I want it for the office or my condo."

I listened to him in a daze. The bigger samples were selling for over $600. Was he aware of that?

Wait, I'm not charging him. That's ridiculous. Although maybe he could help offset the delivery charges...

He looked at me. "Anyway. We can figure that all out later." He took a step toward me. "What I really came here to say is this...I'm so sorry. I disrespected you in the worst manner and regret it more than I can say."

"Okay. Thank you."

He drew even closer. "And...I've missed you terribly."

I swallowed and fought back tears. "I've missed you, too, Nick."

"So...I know you have a rule concerning not giving guys a second chance. And even if you didn't, you've already given me mine when I told you to fuck off in the courtroom."

"It was 'stay the fuck away from me.'"

His mouth slid into a grin. That lopsided grin of his that made my knees weak. "I'm flattered that you memorized my words."

My lips twitched. "You're welcome."

He was serious again. "Bobby Jo, I was a complete jerk. I let someone say something degrading regarding you...although I did set him straight eventually."

"You did?"

He nodded. "But that's really neither here nor there. I should have threatened his life the moment he said one ugly thing about you."

I fought the smirk that was begging to come out. "I don't think threatening his life would have been necessary."

He stared at the floor, pressing the toes of one foot into the hardwood and twisting back and forth like he was extinguishing a cigarette. "Do you think you could find it in your heart to forgive me? Give me one more chance?" He squinted up at me.

I inhaled and exhaled, closing my eyes.

I'd be an idiot to say yes, wouldn't I? But God how I want to.

"That goes against who I am."

His face fell.

He seemed sincere...

"But the who I am now is a lot different from the who I was before I met you," I admitted.

His gaze flashed to my face.

"We'd have to go slow..."

He jumped on that. "Slow as a sloth. I promise."

I wouldn't let him off that easy. "And I'd have some stipulations."

"Why do I feel like Hercules receiving his tasks?"

I ignored that, tilting my head and raising my brows. "You'd have to meet my daddy..."

"Done."

I blinked. "What?"

"Your father and I had a little tête-à-tête before I came here."

My stomach dropped. No telling what my father had done. "Oh? How'd that go?"

"Good. I told him I was here to apologize to you. He said something like 'You go and do that. And when you're done, get your happy ass on out of town.'"

I covered my mouth to try to stop my laughter, but I couldn't.

He put his hands on his hips. "Oh, you think that's funny, huh?"

I regained control. "Sorry."

"Don't be. It's nice to see you laugh." We stared at each other again, communicating without words.

"You'll have to woo me."

"Oh, I will. It'll be the best wooing you've ever seen."

"But you don't have to buy my artwork."

He looked a little panicked. "But I want to."

"You don't have to say that."

"Bobby Jo, I'm not trying to butter you up by buying your work. I really want these pieces, no matter what goes down with us. Seriously." He pulled out his wallet.

It warmed me. It was appropriate that he have the Denver skyline as I'd been thinking about him when I created it.

"I'm not making you pay for them, Nick."

"No way," he said sternly. "I'm guessing it took hours and hours to make these. I'm paying for that, along with your materials, craftsmanship, and artistic talent. Do you take credit cards?"

"This doesn't feel right..."

"Bullshit. I'm not taking them if you don't let me pay. But please don't say you won't, because I have my heart set on them."

I scrunched my nose. "You're serious?"

"Absolutely," he said without hesitating.

"Okay. That'll be four hundred dollars."

He frowned. "Come on. What's the real total? Any single one of those would go for far more than that."

"But they're a lot, Nick."

"I get that. Several thousand per item, I'm sure. But I've saved plenty of money for an occasion such as this. When I want something, I generally get it."

I wasn't sure if he was still talking about my art.

"All right. But they are only $650 for the bigger pieces, and a hundred for the horse."

"You're kidding."

"No, I'm not. Check the price tags."

He did. "Well, shit. I need a few more then."

He took all the others, and a sample of wall art with a wine bottle and glass for one of the partners in his firm. He got very excited by a stag design for his other partner, who he said was obsessed with hunting deer. And he decided to purchase a whimsical one I'd made with a bird wearing a hat. He said his mom would go ape over it. He asked me to hold them for him for a bit.

The door jangled, and a couple entered and began looking at the artwork. Nick eyed them and leaned in. "Can I take you out tomorrow night?"

I smiled. "Pick me up at six."

"Awesome. I'll be here." The couple seemed to have found a piece they liked. "I'll let you get to your customers." He started to walk away, but I called his name and crooked a finger at him.

When he came closer, I said, "We have to do something we've never done."

"You've got it."

"And no physical contact yet. Even holding hands."

He grinned, repeating words he'd said before. "You're going to make me work for this, aren't you?"

I leaned forward so that mere inches separated us. "Damn straight."

"Okay. But you'll be the one who suffers." He left, looking back at me over his shoulder one more time.

I let my gaze travel to his jeans that he filled out so nicely.

But what a delicious form of suffering.

CHAPTER TWENTY-THREE

N*ick*

I was at Huddle House eating lunch. The same four men sat in the same booth as they had the last time I was in. It was like they'd never left. It tickled me for some reason. Only today, they were being quite rowdy. Teasing one poor guy about the size of the deer he shot.

"Well, seein' as y'all don't respect me," he rose with his plate, "I'm gonna go eat with this young fella."

I stopped with my delicious-looking cheeseburger halfway to my mouth as he took a seat opposite me. He smirked at his friends triumphantly.

"Oh, now. Quit pitchin' a hissy fit. Come back over here. And bring that young man with ya. He shouldn't have to eat alone."

"Besides," said another guy at the table, "we want to get to know him." He leaned forward, crossing his arms.

It would have been impolite not to join them, so I shifted my burger and Coke to the end of their table and spun my chair, getting the sense that it had just become the hot seat. I shook with the nearest man. "Hi. Nick Adams."

"Jackson Tate," the first man said. He was tall and slim, with a head of thinning gray hair. He turned to introduce me to his friends. "This here is Beau Brooks, and this is Brooks Hartman." He arched his brows. "And yes, that's confusin' as all get out. But Brooks refuses to change his name to Oliver, for some reason."

The fourth man didn't seem to want to wait for Jackson to introduce him. He extended his hand. "Carter Beamer. Welcome to Harlan."

"Thank you." I waited for conversation to begin again so I could eat my burger, but they just sat back, eyeing me.

I cleared my throat. "So, what do you gentlemen do for a living?"

Jackson again spoke up. He must have been the leader of this little gang. "Me and Brooks work in the mine. Carter's a janitor at the..."

"Harlan Health and Rehabilitation Center," he offered.

"Yeah, that's a mouthful. I always get it wrong." Jackson grabbed Beau by the shoulders roughly. "And ol' Beau, here, he simply lives off the kindness of others."

His face flushed. "I'm currently without a job."

"Yeah," Carter started in. "He's so poor he has a tumbleweed as a pet."

Beau laughed. "I do not." He shrugged. "It's true. I'm broke." He paused. "I'm so broke I can't afford to pay attention." I guess his strategy was to join them and heckle himself.

They all roared. These guys razzed each other like my friends and I did, only with gray hair and a drawl.

Jackson shushed everyone and addressed me. "What do you do for a livin', Nick?"

I had just taken a bite of my burger, so they waited for me to swallow. "I'm a lawyer."

They exchanged a quick look. "Ahh."

"A lawyer, eh?" Beau said contemplatively. "You're probably so rich you bought a new boat because your other one got wet."

Jackson elbowed him, frowning. "Will you quit being ugly? That there is rude." A phone buzzed on the table beside him; he took a peek at it then laid it down, turning to me. "Don't pay him no mind. His brain rattles around like a BB in a box car. You here 'cuz you're workin' with that McCaffrey gal?"

"Not exactly," I hedged. They gazed at me so expectantly, I blurted out, "I came to win her back."

"Well, now," Jackson said in a softer tone than he'd been using. "Y'all have a spat, did ya?"

"Yeah. Totally my fault."

He nodded sympathetically. "We've all been there." He glanced around the table, and they all murmured their agreement. "Hell, Carter's spent so many nights on the couch his Memory Foam mattress done forgot him." They snickered, then Jackson returned his attention to me. "Ya say something stupid, did ya?"

"Not me. But a buddy of mine said something crude about her, and I didn't kick his ass like I should have."

Jackson released a low whistle. "I bet she was madder than a wet hen."

"Not really. She was more...hurt."

"She was sore over it. That's worse."

Beau groaned. "Oh, Lawd, I hate that. I'd rather her rail on me for a month of Sundays than do that blubberin'. I can't take that."

Brooks sat forward suddenly. "Ya got a plan to woo her?"

It felt good talking to someone about it. "Not exactly... What do you do around here for fun?"

"Ya mean when we're not workin' our asses off?" Beau inquired.

"Well, there's the Possum Fest," Brooks offered.

"No, you fool, it's the Poke Sallet Festival. Possum Fest's in October," Jackson corrected.

I felt a surge of relief. I didn't want anything to do with any Possum Festival. Although I had no idea what poke sallet meant.

Jackson rubbed his chin. "Hmm...that ain't a bad idear, even if it came from you," he said to Brooks. "You can get plenty romantic while sharing one of them cotton candy cones."

Really?

Jackson's phone buzzed again. This time he didn't even check it. We all realized at the same time, that the waitress had come over and was waiting for us to stop talking.

"Anybody want a piece of pie? It's strawberry rhubarb today."

Beau waved her off. "Not for me. I'm full as a tick."

"Okay, well here's your ticket. And your ticket." She passed them out. "Who's getting Beau's meal? I'm sure it's not you, Brooks." She looked at me. "He squeezes a quarter so hard the eagle screams." They all sniggered.

I stretched to snatch it from her. "I've got it, and everybody else's too."

"What?" one said.

"Ya don't have to do that," another stated.

"I owe you guys. You gave me that whole pork sallet thing."

The waitress smiled winningly. "That's poke sallet. Don't ya know what poke sallet is, sugar?"

"Ah, now, Daisy," Jackson said right away, "he's a city boy. Don't give him a hard time." He turned to me. "You are from the city, aren't ya, son?"

"Yes. Does it show?"

"Yes," all five of them answered.

And I thought I was blending in.

"Poke sallet," she explained, "is a dish made with poke weed, which is poisonous, so you have to be careful with it. You have to boil it and rinse it real good, and then it's usually cooked in bacon fat with a little onion...whooey! That's some good eatin'. Make ya want to slap your mama."

Everyone else nodded their agreement, but I had my doubts. And why would I slap my mother?

"I'll be back with your change in two shakes of a lamb's tail. Don't you go anywhere now," she said with some pretty intense eye contact.

"Oh, keep the change." At the prices they were charging at the Huddle House, the poor thing could hardly live off tips if people only tipped twenty percent.

"Oh," she blushed. "Thank ya kindly." She threw me a wink, seeming to take the hefty tip as some kind of come on, which it definitely wasn't. I mean she was pretty all right, with short, tight, curly blonde hair and nice features, but she appeared to be at least ten years younger than my twenty-seven, if not more. She sashayed away with an armload of plates from our table, looking at me over her shoulder. My new pals gave some low whistles.

"Well, butter my backside and call me a biscuit. I think the gal's sweet on you," Brooks offered.

I glanced behind me, and she smiled at me. I quickly spun to face the table. "I'm afraid so."

"Yeah," Brooks said slowly. "She's goin' through a divorce and is on the hunt for a little action, I'd say."

I almost spit my soda out. "Divorce? She seems like she's about seventeen."

"That's right," Brooks replied matter-of-factly.

Beau interjected, "Nah. Ya gotta be eighteen to be married. She's eighteen."

Brooks sneered. "Now don't go showin' your ignorance again, Beau." He peered at me. "Half the time he don't know whether to check his ass or scratch his watch." He glared at Beau. "Her mama and daddy signed for her. She's seventeen. She was in my granddaughter's class." He shifted his gaze to her again as she leaned over a bus tub. "Ended up to be halfway good-lookin', too." Addressing me, he added, "She was so ugly when she was born her mama used to borrow a baby to take to church."

Jackson eyed her as well. "That's God's truth."

The door flew open with an angry jangling from the bells above it, and a woman swept into the room with dark curls and an even darker expression. She wore a flowery dress that must have come straight from the fifties.

"Uh-oh," Jackson mumbled, sliding down in his seat. He grabbed a hat from the ledge, jammed it on and tilted it to conceal his face.

"Jackson Emmit Tate," the newcomer railed.

The other three seemed amused. "Oh, that's not good," Brooks commented. "She used your full name."

"You old fool. I've been looking for you all over God's creation." She snatched the hat from his head and hit him with it, messing up his thinning hair comically.

He worked at getting the stray strands back into place. He spoke to me out of the side of his mouth. "This here's my blushing bride. Darlin', this is Nick."

She slid her steely blue eyes from him to me, granting me a faint smile and a quasi-curtsy. "How do?" Without taking a breath, she refocused on Jackson. "You don't know to answer your dang phone?"

"Well, honey," he simpered, "I guess I done left my phone in the car." Her attention shifted and, too late, he saw his phone on the table and slammed his hand on it.

"You're lyin'. You know how I know you're lyin'?" She didn't wait for an answer. "Because your damned lips are moving."

"Whooey!" Beau exclaimed, his gaze dancing with amusement.

Carter tried to hide a chuckle behind his napkin as he pretended to wipe his face.

"Here ya are lah-de-dahing with this gaggle of misfits..." she gestured.

"Hey," Beau commented with a frown.

"You, hush now." She peered at me. "That one thinks the sun come up just to hear him crow." She scowled at him before returning her aim to target number one, her husband. "I'm worn slap out traipsing around hell's half acre, on accoun'a you, as busy as a moth in a mitten, and you're all cozy here, scarfin' down..." she glanced at his plate, "...pancakes! You know the doctor don't want ya eatin' any pancakes."

"That's Beau's plate."

Beau went to defend his friend. “He did actually—”

She extended an arm, palm toward Beau without even looking at him. “Bocifus Alexander Brooks, you best stay clear of this.”

“Yes’m,” he said contritely, waving his hands in submission.

“She knows your name?” Brooks queried in a low voice, his eyes wide.

“Her mama knows my mama...”

“Ahh.” Brooks nodded his understanding.

Daisy chose this moment to reenter the scene, leaning over me unnecessarily to get my glass, practically jamming her breasts in my face. Her blouse was unbuttoned more than it had been earlier, and it was also now tied high on one side, displaying her midriff. All conversation stopped as everyone stared at her, even Jackson’s pissed wife.

“I’ll take care of you, honey.”

She didn’t seem to be talking about my Coke.

After she left, Jackson said as an aside to me, “Let me show you how to make amends with a woman, son.” He straightened, clearing his throat. “Woman. Who licked the red off your candy cane?”

She gasped. “Well, I never!” She narrowed her eyes. “You’re lower than a snake’s belly in a wagon rut.” She threw an arm out. “I’m running hither and yon, busier than a cat trying to bury crap on a marble floor, searchin’ the Walmart to replace your holey-assed underwear—”

Jackson slid down again, with a groan. “Oh, Lawd.”

“What? You don’t want me commenting on your ‘unmentionables’ in front of these morons?”

Carter raised a finger. “Umm...I was valedictorian of my class.”

She rotated her head. “Yes, Carter Christopher Beamer—”

He gasped loudly. “She knows my name!” he yiped like it was the key to his destruction.

Jackson’s wife put her hands on her hips. “You don’t think your Emma talks about you at the beauty parlor?” She nodded knowingly. “She talks about you all right. Talks about you aplenty.”

Carter paled, gaping at her.

She left him to consider all the implications of that, spinning to Jackson momentarily but whirling back. "And we all know you were vale*dic*torian of your class...all two of you. Now zip it."

He followed in Beau's footsteps. "Yes'm." He mimicked zipping his lips, twisting the imaginary lock, and placing the key to it in his pocket.

Jackson's wife, whose name I still didn't know, took a deep breath and reloaded. "Now. As for you, mister...answer your damn phone when I call. You keep doing this crap, I'll cancel your birth certificate."

He brushed it off with a weak laugh.

"Don't you ignore me." She shook her finger at him. "I'll jerk you bald." Daisy had returned with my refill, and Jackson's wife eyed her as she talked. "Don't you go giving me any more of your excuses. I was born at night, but it wasn't last night."

"Ya finished?" Jackson grumbled.

She drew herself up to her full five-foot-two. "I believe I am. You've got one minute for goodbyes. I'll be outside." She nodded at me. "Nice meeting you, Nick." She glared at Daisy balefully. "Good Lord, Daisy. Put some clothes on. You'll catch old and new-monia dressed like that." With that, she spun on her heel and left.

"Why if that don't dill my pickle," Daisy muttered, and she wandered off.

We all stared at each other for a moment, then Beau threw a look over his shoulder. Jackson's wife stood facing down the street, her arms crossed. "You best get goin', Jackson."

He stole a glance too. "Aww. I ain't jumpin' just because she says to jump."

As though she could hear from a twenty-foot distance, through glass, Mrs. "Jackson"—I'd forgotten Jackson's last name—twisted to glare at him.

He hurriedly collected his phone. "But seein' how I was about to leave anyway..." He slid along the booth and got to his feet. "See you boys tomorrow. Nick, come back and let us know how things went."

Not waiting for my response, he darted away and out the door. We watched as his missus started in on him. He hung his head and took it like a man.

"I'm certainly glad he showed me how to handle women," I joked, unsure of how it would be taken.

But the boys cut up. Carter punched me in the shoulder. "You're all right, Nick."

"Thanks." I chuckled. "Boy, he left in a hurry, didn't he?"

Brooks stretched and spoke while yawning. "Ya got that right. Usually, it's like herding turtles to get Jackson to leave here. Well, I best follow suit and get the hell home before Cindy waltzes in here in her housecoat."

We all rose and said our goodbyes.

"Does this town have a florist?"

Beau pointed in the direction that Jackson and his wife had disappeared in. "Just around the corner. Ya can't miss it."

"Thanks."

As we walked toward the door, he rested his hand on my shoulder. "Flowers, huh? Nice touch. Cindy gets real friendly when I bring home flowers, if you know what I mean." He elbowed me with a chuckle. "In fact, I think I'll join you."

And he did. Luckily, he chose something quickly and left, because I would have been embarrassed by the extravagant bouquet I bought. But I figured I probably had a whole lot more making up to do than he did. I went back to my hotel and showered and got ready for our date. I had a terrible time deciding what one should wear to a Poke Sallet Festival. I finally chose a blue linen shirt and khakis, the first outfit I tried on after going through almost every article of clothing I'd brought with me.

I was uncharacteristically nervous when I arrived at her place. My palms were sweating. I shook my head and laughed at myself. I could appear before a judge or give an interview for the five o'clock news with the equanimity of a hippie. But with this woman...

Man. I can't believe the effect she has on me.

Just as I reached for the doorknob, I heard the oddest noise. It sounded like a mix between a dragon breathing, a jet airplane taking off in the distance, and bacon frying in a skillet. Loud initially but settling down into a consistent sizzling noise. Curious, I set the vase of flowers on the stoop and crossed the lawn to peek around the corner of the house. I was not prepared for what I saw on the driveway.

Initially, I was taken aback by the figure in a brown jumpsuit with a helmet on. Then I recognized that they were standing in front of a worktable of sorts and when they changed positions, I caught sight of the welding torch they were wielding. It was her. My dream girl. My fantasy girl. My Bobby Jo. I smiled and watched her for a while, finally clearing my throat. "Umm...Bobby Jo?"

She continued working, focused on her creation. It warmed me, in more than one way, to see her dedication to her art. After a few seconds, she must have sensed my presence because she whirled her head. I felt like I was staring into the eyes of the Black Knight. Until she jumped, and her mumbled voice came from within that hood. "Nick. Oh, my gosh!" She set down her torch and dropped her gloves like a hockey player; they landed at her feet on the drive. Whipping off her hood she threw that thick mane of her hair back in an arc. Something about it really turned me on. I don't know if it was the whole beautiful woman hidden behind a plain coverall or what it was, but my engines were fired, as hot and dangerous as her welding torch. "What time is it?"

"Uhh...a little after six."

Her gaze widened. "Oh. I'm so sorry. I lost track of time." She unzipped her suit a bit. "I just need to take a quick shower and—"

She didn't finish her sentence because I grabbed her and swung her up against the house, crushing her mouth with mine. She groaned, digging her hands in my hair and returning my fervor with her own searing heat. I gripped her waist as my lips cruised along her neck.

She arched. "Oh, Nick. I've missed you."

"Mmm."

And I've missed you. So much it's driving me crazy to be with you now. I yanked at her jumpsuit, forcing the zipper open more, and sunk my teeth into her exposed skin.

"Oh, Nick. Nick," she panted, heating my blood all the more. "Nick...you need to stop."

With regret, I remembered my promise not to touch her. I withdrew, looking off to the side. "I...I'm sorry. I...I don't know what came over me." I slapped my forehead, trying to calm my racing heart. "I got carried away. I didn't mean to—"

She put a finger on my mouth. "Shh. I only meant that I didn't want to give my neighbor a free peep show. We should take this inside." Her eyes glowed intensely. She turned and, skirting her worktable, rushed along the driveway bordering the side of her house, dragging me with her. When she came around the back corner of the house, her strides began to slow, until she halted altogether on the steps leading to her screened-in porch, her hand on the doorknob.

"Is something wrong?"

She spun slowly, resting her arms loosely on my shoulders, and her face was so pained it stung me. Tears began to slide down her cheek. "I'm sorry, Nick. I want to. I do. I just..." Her bottom lip quivered as she searched for words.

"You don't trust me."

She peered behind me somewhere. "It's not that, exactly..."

I lowered my gaze, hunting for a way of expressing myself too. Before I could speak, she jumped in.

"I'm sorry. I didn't mean to lead you on. I thought I could... I wanted to..."

I took a step up, taking her hands. "This is not your fault, it's mine. I told you I would take things slow, and then I practically jumped your bones on your driveway." I was pissed at myself for my lack of self-control. I wiped her tears with my thumb. "Don't cry, honey. I'm sorry."

She slid into my arms, laying her head on my chest.

"I hurt you, and that kills me." I held her, but a few moments later, I chuckled. "I've never given a damn whether the things I did hurt someone or not." I separated from her so that I could peer into her face. "See what you've done to me, Bobby Jo McCaffrey. You've turned me into some sort of...human."

She laughed at that and pulled me close again.

"You've made me so upstanding, I don't know if I can still be a lawyer."

She chuckled from my chest.

I hesitated, afraid to pose my next question. "Do you still want to go to the Pork Sallet Festival with me?"

She leaned back to look at me. "We're going to the *Poke* Sallet Festival?"

"Uhh...yeah. Unless you don't want to," I added hurriedly.

She narrowed her eyes on me but didn't speak.

"Yeah. That was a dumb idea, wasn't it? It's just...Jackson said it was fun."

She spun to head into the house, and I scrambled after her. "Jackson Tate? You're not listening to that ol' fool, are you? He wouldn't have the good sense to come in from the rain."

I grinned. She was showing her Harlan.

"The only reason he suggested it," she continued, "is because his wife is this year's committee chair."

"Uhh...well, it was actually Brooks who suggested it."

"Brooks?" She snorted. "Brooks is a piece of work. The porch light's on with that one, but there ain't *nobody* home." She dragged out the word.

We were standing in a small but sunny kitchen. To the right was a bathroom and a bedroom with the door open. It was even tinier than the kitchen. From where I was standing it looked like the bed was the sole furniture in it, and the mattress was almost rubbing against the window's frame.

"Well, we could do something else..."

She whirled. "Don't be silly. I love the Poke Sallet Festival." She grabbed my face and squeezed it, saying in a weird voice, "And you're so sweet to take me there." She gave me a smacking kiss. "I need to take a quick shower." She was unzipping her coverall then shrugging out of the sleeves. All she had underneath was a black sports bra. She fanned herself. "I'm sweaty. But I'll make it quick. Oh—" She froze.

"Oh, what?"

"I didn't put my stuff away."

"By stuff you mean your artwork, and the tools you used to create it?"

"Yeah." She wheeled around to leave.

I caught her elbow. "I've got it."

She hesitated. "Are you sure?"

I kissed her on the forehead and released her. "I think I can manage it."

"Just stick it in the garage." She went to shower, and I made my way to her work area.

Piece by piece I lugged her tools and artwork to the detached garage, wondering how she ever did it on her own and getting a little sweaty myself. I ran to the front to get my flowers and brought them into the kitchen. I was washing some sort of residue from her artwork off my palms when she reentered.

"Oh, did you get some on you?" She rushed over.

"I don't think so." I dried my hands and turned, examining my clothing. She was wearing a sleeveless, denim-like top with matching shorts, both embroidered with flowers. So not the courtroom B.J. "You look nice."

Her lips lifted at the edges. "Now you're buttering me up."

"No." I smirked. "That's what those are for." I gestured to the ginormous bouquet of red and pink roses and other flowers on the tiny kitchen table.

She spun and gasped, but when she swung back, she narrowed her eyes on me like a witness on the stand. "Did you think you could lure me in with flowers?"

A new layer of sweat gathered. "Well, no...I-I—"

"Well, you're right. You can." She linked her fingers behind my neck. "I love flowers."

"Hmm..." I gave her a fake frown. Because how could I really frown with her in my arms?

She smiled. "They're beautiful." She kissed me lightly, and her gaze lingered on my mouth.

For a few seconds, all I could hear was my heartbeat. I sighed. "We should probably get going."

"Yeah, I suppose we should," she said, but she brushed her lips over mine.

My body tightened. "Bobby Jo," I said as a warning, my voice a low growl.

She separated from me a little, blinking with wide eyes. "Am I teasing you?"

"What do you think?" I said wryly.

She stared at me for a few more seconds. "Don't you think you deserve it?" Her mouth twitched.

"Undoubtedly," I answered immediately. "But I'm still begging you to stop."

She laughed, twirling away from me and grabbing her purse off the chair. "I guess the makeup sex will have to wait until later then." She cut through the swinging door and was gone.

She's playing with me. Like a cat with a mouse. I wish she'd go for the kill already.

I exhaled, amused but still pretty worked up. I held onto the top rung of a kitchen chair for support.

She stuck her head back in. "Are you coming?" she said innocently.

How I wish.

"Give me a second." My voice was rough.

Sliding over, she took my elbow. "Oh, come on, counselor. You'll live."

"I'm not so sure."

I let her drag me out the door.

CHAPTER TWENTY-FOUR

B*obby Jo*

On the way to the festival, I thought through things. When we got downtown and parked, I put my hand on Nick's arm before he got out. "Nick...can I say something?"

He seemed apprehensive. "Of course."

"I want to apologize for leaving Denver without saying goodbye and for not giving you a chance to make amends. I acted like a silly schoolgirl running back home."

"That's okay," he said slowly. "I understand. I acted like a jerk, you had no commitment to me, so if you wanted to come home, who could blame you?"

I lowered my head, irked that I couldn't let it go. "So, you see this—what we have going on between us—as a noncommitted relationship?" When I lifted my gaze, his mouth was hanging open in utter shock.

Why did I have to ask? Why did I have to push things? Why can't I just enjoy spending time together?

"You know, never mind. Let's forget I said anything. Let's go get us some poke sallet," I said with forced cheerfulness. I turned to my door, but he grasped my arm.

"Wait." When I spun to him, he took my hands. "When I said you weren't committed to me," he said in the same slow way, "I meant...you didn't owe me anything."

I suddenly felt like a caged animal. "Okay. Great. I'm glad we straightened that out." I again tried to open my door.

"Bobby Jo."

I reluctantly twisted my head to look at him.

"Listen," he licked his lips, "I'm not certain exactly what's going on between us. All I know is that...I was miserable when you were gone. I drove across the country to find you. I wouldn't drive across town for any other woman. That has to say something." He rubbed his thumb along my fingers, and I watched it glide over my skin. "Hey." He put a fist under my chin and lifted my face. "I want this to work, Bobby Jo." He kissed me tenderly, and I felt my heart slip away when he pulled back. "Better?"

I nodded rapidly, working up a smile.

"Okay. One more thing..."

"Yes?"

"Is it really necessary to eat poke sallet—that sounds like a children's game, by the way—at the Poke Sallet Festival?"

I stared at him. "Is it necessary to eat poke sallet at the Poke Sallet Festival? Yes, city boy, it is. Now let's go."

His making a joke made it better somehow. But as I got out of the car, a thought hit me. Maybe that's what it was supposed to do, distract. Maybe it was one of those tricks in his playboy bag of goodies. I shook my head.

Stop it. You're being ridiculous.

I don't know why I was being so insecure. It wasn't like me. But maybe it was because this had become important to me. He had become important. Was he one of those things a coal miner's kid could never have?

I've proven people wrong before... Sure, he is a playboy. But maybe I'm the girl who'll change that.

Then he came around the side of the car, and I eyed him. Chiseled features, an air of self-confidence that bordered on arrogance, great hair, a phenomenal body...the bastard even smelled good.

Get real, Bobby Jo. Maybe some girl will change him one day, but you're not that girl.

The thousands of times my father had called me worthless and homely, incompetent...they all came crashing in at once. Then, like I always did, I fought them off.

I may not be Nick's girl, but I'm not the girl my father said I was either.

Still hanging on to the car door's handle, I closed my eyes, took a deep, slow breath in through my nose and straightened my shoulders.

You're here to have fun and enjoy the company of an attractive man. It's nothing more than that.

The trick to getting by for Bobby Jo McCaffrey was shooting for the stars but hoping for the horizon. It was a delicate balancing act. Being confident, while guarding my heart, making sure I didn't expect more than I deserved. Being ambitious and self-confident but, at the same time, being realistic. Using my skills in the courtroom and tamping down the little girl screaming inside of me.

"Are you okay?" he murmured, closer than I expected.

I jumped and rallied. "Oh, yes. Just spacing out. Let's get you some pork sallet." I stuck my arm through his.

He laughed. "You said pork sallet."

"I did not!" I said, aghast. I rewound and gasped. "Oh, shit. I did, didn't I?"

He nodded.

I slugged him in the shoulder. "Look what you're doing to me. How will I hold my head up at the Huddle House?"

"I don't know." He chuckled, and I had one of those moments with him where my heart squeezed, and I wanted it to go on forever.

We strode hand in hand to the entrance. "Wow." He was taking in all the activity within the roped off area, the noise of the crowd, and the carnival rides making it necessary for him to raise his volume. "This is a pretty big thing."

"Oh, yes." When we were inside, I elaborated. "On top of the rides and booths here there's music, a run, a car show..." Someone walked by with an iguana in a T-shirt and hat, "...pet show, Poke Sallet Idol, a wrestling tournament, golf tournament..." As a trio of girls passed us with sashes across their chests, I added, "Oh, and a Miss Harlan County Pageant."

"No, kidding?" He turned his head to watch the young ladies.

I elbowed him. "Stop. They're babies."

"What? I was just checking out their sashes."

"More like their asses. Come on, you reprobate." I urged him forward.

Half an hour later, we had our order of poke sallet.

"Wow, it looks...great," he said sarcastically.

"It's not about looks; it's about taste. Take a bite."

He eyed me as if weighing whether this relationship was worth the sacrifice of his tastebuds.

I frowned. "Eat it."

He shoved the fork in his mouth and chewed, grimacing. "It's...good."

I stared at him blandly, a hip cocked. "You may spit it out."

He immediately leaned over a trash barrel and ejected the food.

"Jackson's hearing about this." I walked off.

"Oh, no. Please," he begged, catching me and grabbing my elbow.

We ambled through the festival grounds, and it was nice, really nice to have company for a change. I stopped outside a tent where a band was playing a Rascal Flatts song I liked. I sang a few bars, slowing my steps.

He nodded his head toward the tent. "Let's go in."

"Oh, no. We don't have to. There's a Kiss tribute band you'll probably like." I started to lead him away.

He grinned. "Come on."

He tugged me, reluctantly, onto the dance floor, where two couples were, locked together in the steady rhythm of a slow dance, and drew me into his arms. My heart fluttered, but I batted it aside. I looked around, uncomfortable.

"What are you doing?"

"Seeing if anyone I know's here."

"Why? Are you embarrassed to be with me?"

My gaze flew to his face. "No. Of course not. Why would I be?"

He shrugged. "You tell me."

"It's not that. I don't want people to see..."

How infatuated I am with you. That'll make it hurt more when you leave. It'll give them something else to laugh at me about, like my mismatched, mis-sized clothes in school, or my daddy's behavior at the local tavern.

"Don't want them to see what? Us dancing together?"

"No." I peered at him, and suddenly, none of it mattered. "I don't want them to ruin this for us." *True.* Although I felt stupid saying it.

"No one's ruining this for us, Bobby Jo. I won't let them."

My heart swelled painfully in my chest, and I blinked back tears. "That's nice of you to say."

He looked from one of my eyes to the other. "I'm not just saying it."

Oh, God. How I wish that were true.

And I let the thought hang there. I didn't swat it away or push it down, knowing full well that I had no business wishing it.

He made a show of glancing around. "Do you think they'd boot us if I kissed you?"

Over his shoulder, a couple were going at it hard, swapping spit. I nodded in their direction. "I don't think so."

"Good." He held his arm up so that I could twirl under it, and I thought he was leading me on, until he pulled me against his body and lowered his lips to mine. The kiss was soft and sweet. It felt so real. He lifted my hair in the back, tilting my head more so that he could take the kiss deeper.

This will kill me.

When he drew away, he searched my face. "What's wrong?"

"Nothing. I'm just...a little hot. Do you think we could go get a lemon shake-up?"

"Of course. Anything you want." As we ducked under the edge of the tent, he asked, "What's a lemon shake-up? Is that like a lemonade?"

I stopped in my tracks. "Who are you? You don't know what a lemon shake-up is? It's not like you're from New York City; you're from Nebraska, for goodness sake. Surely, you've had a lemon shake-up at the Nebraska State Fair."

"I've never been."

"Never been? What did you do as a kid?"

His eyes glowed, and he opened his mouth to answer my question, but I curtailed that.

"Wait. I don't want to hear." We arrived at a food truck. "A lemon shake-up is lemon wedges, sugar, and ice that is shaken."

"So, like lemonade."

"Yes. We'll take two lemon shake-ups. And...do you want to split a funnel cake?"

I looked at him, and he stared at me blankly.

"So help me God, if you say you don't know what a funnel cake is..."

He was getting his wallet out. "No. Of course, I know what a funnel cake is." Then he "whispered" to the woman helping us, "What's a funnel cake?"

"Well, I'm gonna ed-ja-ma-kate you right now."

He grabbed my hips. "Ooh. I like it when you talk all scholarly."

I laughed and slapped at his hands. "Stop it."

He quit and gave the girl two twenties. He leaned so he could check the menu. "Is that enough?"

"More than enough," she answered, giving him a twenty back. "Do you want anything on your funnel cake?"

"Umm...I'm not sure." He turned to me. "Do we want anything on our funnel cake?"

I glared at him. "Heathen." I addressed the lady in the trailer. "Hot fudge and whipped cream, please." She was eyeing Nick a little too openly, so I gave her some eye of my own, and she scurried off.

Nick noticed. "What did you say to her?" He dropped the twenty into her tip jar.

"Nothing," I said sweetly.

He studied me. "Hmm."

When we got our treat, we walked and ate, in the hopes of burning like fifty of the two thousand calories we were eating. We came to the game booths.

"Step right up. Step right up. Win the lady a prize." It was Jackson Tate.

Nick sidled over with a frown. "You telling me to go to the festival didn't have anything to do with your wife being head of the festival committee, did it?"

Jackson feigned ignorance. "Oh, is she? I didn't know that."

Nick sneered, setting his cup on the ground and digging out his wallet again. "Did you make peace with her, by the way? She seemed pretty steamed."

"What? Her?" He waved his hand, seeming completely unaware that she was approaching behind him. "That woman could argue with an empty house."

"Oh? What woman is that?" she asked pointedly.

"Why..." He looked at Nick with comic desperation. "Your ma, m'dear."

"Well, that's God's truth."

Jackson wiped his brow exaggeratedly.

"But not your wife, huh, husband?"

He put up his hands in a gesture of innocence. "What?"

She gave Nick some baseballs in exchange for his bill.

"So, what do I have to do?"

"Just throw these," she waved an arm deeper into the booth, "and knock over those milk bottles."

"Oh, is that all?" He threw three balls and made three misses. "What the hell? I knew I'd be rusty, but this is ridiculous." He rolled his sleeves aggressively. He knocked one down with the next pitch and missed with his last two."

"Ahh...now," Jackson drawled. "That's a shame. But you do get this consolation prize."

Nick scoffed, slipping his wallet out again. "I don't want that damn thing. Give me six more balls." The next round produced similar results.

I tugged on his sleeve. "Nick. It doesn't matter."

"No. I'm winning you a prize." He looked at Jackson who was about to offer him the little teddy bear again. "A real prize. Six more." After a bit, a crowd had gathered to watch the crazy man going after the milk jugs.

"You're going to pull something," I warned. He wasn't listening.

Seventy-five dollars later, he proudly handed me a practically life-sized stuffed bear that would take up more of my bed than I was willing to give.

I thanked him then asked if he was ready to go.

He grinned. "Hell, yeah. This place is bleeding me dry." He put his arm over my shoulder.

"Well, you didn't have to win this..."

"Of course I did."

"I would have been fine with a smaller one."

"Nonsense. My girl's got to have the best."

His girl?

We got to his Maserati, oddly enough, the sole Maserati on the square, and he walked around to his side.

"I'm just saying, we could have purchased a room full of stuffed animals with that seventy-five dollars."

"But I wouldn't have won them," he said matter-of-factly.

"True. Still..."

"Where to now? Or do you want to go back and watch the pageant?" He made a move to open his door, but I grabbed him.

"The only girl in skimpy clothing that you'll be ogling tonight is me."

He leaned over to kiss me. "Ooh. I like the sound of that." As we kissed, he revved the engine, making me laugh.

"Come on. Let's go." After a moment or two, he said thoughtfully, "I bet those baseballs were rigged."

CHAPTER TWENTY-FIVE

N*ick*

I parked in front of her place.

"Would you like to come in?"

Hell, yeah. "Sure."

"I might have some wine. Are you hungry? I can probably make something if you're hungry." Her words came out rushed. She was nervous. I needed to take things slow.

"I noticed you have a swing in the back." It was one of those porch swings but not on her porch, supported by a framework. "Would you like to take our wine there and maybe talk for a while?"

She seemed to relax from her smile down. "That sounds nice."

She found a bottle of pinot noir, and I opened it for her. She'd disappeared, so I rummaged in the cabinets, finally shouting, "Where are your wineglasses?"

Unbeknownst to me, she'd snuck up behind me. "Wineglasses? What do you think this place is, city boy? The Ritz?" She grabbed the bottle and chugged some.

"Works for me."

She'd ditched her shoes, and so was barefoot as she crossed her patchy lawn. It made me wonder if she ran around that way as a little girl, and I smiled. She moved with the same grace as she did in high heels.

She held the chain the swing was suspended from as she sat. "I still can't believe you've never been to the state fair."

I shrugged as I sat beside her. "I guess it wasn't something we did. The one time Zack and Zoe did go— because one of her favorite bands was playing there— I was sick and had to miss."

"That's too bad," she murmured, taking a drink then passing the bottle to me.

"I talk about Zoe too much, don't I?"

"No, no." But she stared at her lap. "She was a huge part of your life. You're still grieving. It's only natural." When she did lift her gaze, I felt like she was watching my reaction to her statement.

I took a drink to give me time to think over my response. "I suppose you're right." I sighed, playing with her fingers with my free hand. "But that doesn't mean I need to drag that baggage into our relationship."

"I don't mind." She grinned wickedly. "It proves you have a heart, counselor."

And right now, it's beating for no one but you, counselor.

"That's what I like about you. I like the way you've been giving me shit all night long because I never went to the fair."

She smirked. "You like that, huh? What other qualities of mine do you like?" she teased, but I considered the answer seriously.

"I like to watch you in action. Whether that's in the courtroom or creating your art. That kind of passion and talent is sexy."

"It is?" She glowed.

"Very much so. I like how you say what's on your mind. Most people hide behind a bunch of bullshit. Hell, I hide behind a bunch of bullshit. But you don't. It's brave."

Instead of pumping her up, the statement seemed to deflate her some. "I'm not so sure of that."

"Well, I am." I twisted to set the wine bottle on a wicker table beside me. "And I like the way you kiss. I especially like that." I leaned in and took her lips softly but eased off, wanting to see where she'd take things. She withdrew, and my heart sank. Then she bent her knees and wrapped her arms around them.

"I'm not always brave," she murmured.

"Oh," I responded gently.

She looked me in the eye. "I'm afraid of how I'll feel when you leave."

"Oh." I hadn't even thought of that. All I had on my mind was winning her back. And I didn't want to think about leaving now, either.

It was quiet, just the squeak of the chains holding the swing, and crickets chirping in the grass somewhere nearby. While the day had been warm, the night was beautiful. A gentle breeze fanned us, and the stars were out in abundance. The sky was still light enough that I could distinguish the mountain range. I nodded in its direction. "Are those the Cumberlands or the Appalachians?"

"What?" Noting my line of vision, she turned her head. A funny little smile crossed her lips. "Oh, they're both." Seeing my confusion, she elaborated. "The Cumberland Mountains are part of the Appalachians."

Not taking my gaze from her, I commented, "They're beautiful."

She sighed. "Yeah, I guess they are. They're different from the Rockies."

"You know, from what you said, I expected the air to be heavy here, but it's not."

She signaled for the bottle. "That's because there isn't much mining anymore. Ironically— or not ironically, depending on how you look at it— I heard the biggest industry in town these days is the health industry. The mining might have dwindled, but its effects didn't." She passed me the bottle and focused on the mountains again. "I'm worried about my dad." She faced me, and her brow was furrowed. "Did he cough a lot when you saw him?"

"No."

"Hmm."

"But," I admitted, "I wasn't there more than a couple of minutes before he kicked me out."

"Mmm." She stared off to the side, lost in thought.

I shook the bottle. "Do you have any more?"

"I'm afraid not."

I yawned. "Probably for the best. I should get going." I rose. "Do you want—"

She grabbed my hand, and I twisted. She was still sitting on the swing. Her eyes were moist for some reason, and her words were choked. "Don't leave."

Did she really say that, or am I fantasizing? "What?"

She seemed panicked. "Stay. Please, stay, Nick."

I immediately sat beside her. "Honey..." I found myself choked up, too. I caressed her cheek. "If you don't want me to go then I'm not leaving. They'd have to drag my dead body out of here to make me go."

She laughed, which is what I'd hoped for. I kissed her brow and held her against my chest for a moment. She melted into me, and it felt so right. I drew back, grasping her biceps and ducking to get a clear view of her face. "Are you sure?"

She nodded her head vigorously. "Make love to me."

Her voice still had that begging quality, which bugged me, but I wasn't about to say anything regarding it at the moment. Instead, I kissed her then stood and offered her my hand. We walked slowly, knowing we were on the verge of doing something that would change things for us. But then I was flooded with a wave of joy. I would make her mine. I stopped and released her hand.

She spun, looking afraid that I was changing my mind.

Not a chance.

"What?"

I bent and swept her off her feet.

She giggled, scrambling to hold on to me. "What are you doing?"

"If we're doing this, we're doing it right." I kissed her as we made our way, but when we got to the door, I was at a loss as to how I was supposed to get it open. I shifted her in my arms and kind of rested her on my knee. I pulled the door open wide, but before I could readjust her, it closed. "Well, fuck. How do they do this in the movies?"

She laughed. "Set me down, you idiot."

"There's no need for name calling."

She led me through her kitchen, turning to smile at me. "Come on." When she got to the bedroom door, she walked backwards, tugging me by both hands. I tackled her, and we fell on the bed.

"Ooh." She pressed up on her elbows. "I'm not sure if this old bed can take that."

"Well, it might as well break now, because what we're about to do will wipe it out for certain." I put my palm on the side of her face and stretched to kiss her. Next thing I knew, we were whipping off our clothes. My shirt was gone in seconds, and I unbuckled my belt. I went to give her a quick glance, merely to check on her progress, but I froze. I could not take my eyes from her.

She was standing by the side of the bed in her bra and underwear. I took in her body, and it was amazing. But that was a fleeting, even trivial, realization. My focus was locked on her face. I was filled with the strangest sensation. It was like when I would be putting together a jigsaw puzzle, and one of the integral pieces fell to the floor, and was lost for a time, then I found it. It fit perfectly, and it made the rest into something beautiful that made sense. It was so odd, but I knew, I knew in a way that I had never known anything before, that my real life began and ended with her. She was it. A complicated woman who had, like that puzzle piece, all sorts of interesting angles. I was struck, in awe of this miracle that God had given me.

I sat and moved to the edge of the bed. My throat was so dry and tight I could hardly speak, but I struggled out, "Come here." She came to me, and I separated my knees. My hands were trembling when I grasped her hips and led her between my legs, all while still looking into her face. Eventually, my mind remembered that I was supposed to be doing something, and I slowly lowered my gaze to her stomach and kissed it. I was so overcome with emotion that I twisted my head, laying my cheek against her smooth skin and clutching her tighter.

She didn't say anything, just played with my hair in a soothing way. Regaining my composure, I drew back, but it was like I didn't know where to start. To my surprise, she knelt before me, and I realized that was what I wanted. I wanted her on my level so that I could see her better. I stroked her hair then ran my hand along her cheek to her chin. Slowly I lowered my lips to hers and kissed her deeply, almost reverently, a coupling of our mouths to foreshadow what was to come. I'm not certain how long we stayed like that—several minutes?—neither one of us was in a hurry.

After a time, I grasped her underneath her elbows and helped her to her feet as I stood. "Umm...could you...lay down, please." I had lost all finesse; there was no smoothness in my actions whatsoever, but I was fully in the moment.

She looked at the bed then at me, a question in her eyes, showing the first little sign of unease, wondering, I'm sure, what was wrong with me. But she opened herself to me, stretching across the bed and watching me. I slowly and deliberately unbuttoned and unzipped my pants, shedding all my clothes. She had sheer curtains, anyone could have seen into the room. We'd have to do something about that. The streetlight, or moonlight, or whatever, filtered in and gave us the perfect amount of light.

I crawled up her body, grasped her wrists, and swept them above her head, holding them against the mattress. We began our kisses again, soul-searing and unhurried. Nothing could have torn us from that bed. We were so into each other, totally absorbed in our lovemaking. It was unlike anything I'd done before. Perfect. Her breath in my ear, the sound, the heat, the way she undulated against mine, in rhythm, synced with my every movement... At one point, I took my weight from her, and stretched out on my side, gliding my hands over her skin, touching her everywhere. There was very little talking but lots of communication. As it was happening, I was hyperaware that this would never happen again. We'd make love again, I hoped, but it would never be exactly like this moment in time.

We finished as we'd begun. When she got close to the end, I slowed, one exquisite push and retreat at a time. Not in screaming need. But we needed each other all the same. As she came down, I kissed her neck as a final statement of my love for her, because that's what it was. I loved her completely. I'd either win, and everything would be bliss, or I'd lose, and be destroyed. But I was all in.

I sat with my back against the wall, as she had only a frame, box springs, and mattress. She slipped an arm through mine and hugged it to her chest like a teddy bear, her cheek warming the skin of my shoulder as she fell asleep. She lay like that for a long time. My opposite elbow was bent, my hand behind my head. I watched the sway of the trees, and a clothesline with nothing but pins outside the window. A car's lights shone straight into the room then swung away, as her house was on the corner, and someone had turned.

I thought about how strange it was that I was in a bedroom with the paint chipping off the window frame, in Harlan, Kentucky, of all places. It was a far cry from my posh condo in Denver. My closet at home was considerably bigger than the bedroom I was in. There were no five-star restaurants here, no high-class gyms with swanky spas, mine was the only luxury car in town. But I liked it here. Felt perfectly comfortable and at home. Nothing was lacking. But in Denver, when she was gone, something essential was missing, and it dragged me down a little more each day. Her.

"Nick," she mumbled.

"Hmm?"

"Can't you sleep?"

"I was just thinking."

Her eyes were shut, and she smiled. "Think closer to me."

I grinned. We were already glued to each other's sides. "Oh, I'm not close enough for you?" I teased. I slid down and turned onto my side, pulling her into me tightly. She squirmed, and I loosened my grip. She flopped onto her side, too, and I encircled her around her chest. She snuggled her little tush in nearer, again hugging my arm, reaching from underneath. My cheek was against hers. I lifted my head to kiss her face then settled in. She sighed, and we drifted off to sleep together.

Sun poured in the window and onto the worn, soft as cream quilt, whose patches were so faded the colors couldn't be distinguished. I decided I liked it a whole lot more than my almost $15,000 silk comforter (I was an idiot). I loved that comforter and would have told anyone a week ago that nothing in the world was better. Now I would trade it and the matching silk sheets for this quilt, torn, with pieces of fabric flapping back and forth or missing. I took my first waking breath and inhaled the wonderful fragrance of coffee. Not my seven-buck Caffé Americano from the coffee shop in my condo building, but it was rich-smelling and heavenly. When I opened my eyes, my hand was on her pillow, and she was gone. She would have had to climb over me to leave, as the bed was pushed against the wall, so I was shocked I hadn't woken up. I could hear noises from the kitchen.

I jumped out of bed and tugged my pants on, putting my shirt on as I went to the kitchen. She was at the counter working on something, facing the opposite direction, in denim cutoffs and a T-shirt. The sight of her filled me with warmth.

"Good morning."

She jumped and twisted, covering her heart. "Oh, you scared me. Did I wake you?"

No. But I wish you had.

"I don't think so. What time is it?"

She glanced at the microwave. "Eight-fifteen. How'd you sleep?" She placed a plate of bacon on the table, and I noticed her hands were trembling.

I crossed to her and encircled her waist, but she kept her arms between us. "Like a king. You're shaking. Did I scare you that bad?"

"Yeah, I guess so," she said hurriedly. She pulled away and went to the stove. "Do you want some eggs?"

"Sure," I said slowly, trying to determine what was going on with her.

"It won't take long. I have everything ready. Why don't you take a seat?"

I drew out a chair and lowered myself into it, still watching her as she poured something into a skillet. "Is everything all right?"

"Of course. Orange juice?" Her voice wasn't pitched right.

I frowned, still attempting to read her. "Yeah. That sounds good."

When she put it on the table, I grabbed her hand before she could leave. "What's wrong?" I asked softly.

"Nothing, *counselor*," she sniped.

Her tone hurt and angered me. "Hey. I'm not asking in a lawyer way. I'm concerned."

She hung her head. "I'm sorry." This time, she didn't try to move away.

"Come here." I pulled her into my lap. "Did I do something wrong last night?"

She smiled at that. "No. Definitely no."

Good to know.

"Well...are you mad because I slept so long?"

"No, Nick. I wanted you to get your sleep."

"But...?"

"I wasn't sure...if I should wake you up or not."

Okay? What is that supposed to mean? That stumped me. While I puzzled over that, she ran a palm across my shoulder as if ironing out a wrinkle.

"I didn't know...if you were leaving today."

"Oh." The grip on my chest lightened. "No, I'm not leaving." I bracketed her face with my hands. "We have all day together." I kissed her. "Unless you have some work to do..."

She smiled wryly. "No. Business isn't exactly booming, as you can see."

"Is that part of what's worrying you? Because as soon as they see what a kickass lawyer you are, they'll be knocking down your door."

She hopped up suddenly. "Oh, shoot! Your eggs."

I twisted back to the table and had a drink of juice. "So...what do you want to do today?"

"I'm game for anything." She seemed much more relaxed when she brought me a plate of eggs and sat. "Oh, toast." She got to her feet, lowered the lever on the toaster, and took her seat again.

"I'm clueless as to what there is to do around here. Is there something that you want to show me? Or...someplace to hike? Or—"

"I know. I'll take you to Kingdom Come State Park, and we can hike there."

The toast popped up, and she started to rise, but I kept her from moving. "I can get it."

"Oh...okay." She seemed a little uncomfortable at first with me working in her kitchen but making plans for the day distracted her.

After breakfast, I went back to my room to shower and change then returned to get her. She'd ordered sandwiches and put together some other food for us to eat on the trail, so our first stop was Huddle House.

CHAPTER TWENTY-SIX

Bobby Jo

Being with Nick had been incredible. Of course, I'd expected him to know his way around the bedroom. A guy like him would. But when he acted so tenderly...I could see why girls would think that he authentically cared for them. I didn't let myself go there. That would be a dangerous place. I was already preparing myself for the sledgehammer of him leaving, which would be the end of everything. It had been great to have him here, but it wouldn't last. He'd go back to Denver, and my little bedroom would be a memory soon erased by other women and other bedrooms.

But at least I had today.

When we walked into Huddle House, the usual characters were present. Jackson Tate hailed us. "Hey there, Romeo."

A huge grin slid across Nick's face. It amused me that he'd made friends with these old men. "Do you mind if we say hi?"

"Not at all." I led the way to the table. They were all cracking up. Curious as to why, I threw a glance over my shoulder. Nick was swaggering behind me, hands clenched above his head, and he was swinging them from side to side like a victorious prize fighter with each exaggerated step, almost like a dance.

I rolled my eyes.

What a ham.

But it warmed me, and I felt a swell of pride in entering with him.

"Well, now. Ain't you bright-eyed and bushy-tailed? Y'all have a nice evenin', did ya?" Jackson's face glowed with humor.

His wife elbowed him lightly in the ribs. "Oh, hush your mouth, you old geezer." She addressed me. "Well, don't you just look pretty as a picture this morning, Bobby Jo?" She may have been a bit more subtle in her statement, but it was obviously laced with innuendo, too, as I was wearing jeans and a T-shirt, having changed for the hike.

"What are ya prattlin' on about, woman? The gal is wearing dungarees and a T-shirt," Jackson countered. "She ain't in no dress-up clothes."

This, of course, earned him another elbow...this one heartier. "Oh, don't you mind him, sugar. You give him two nickels for a dime, he'd think he was rich."

But Jackson wouldn't be stymied. He nodded at Nick. "I see you've been busier than a cat on a hot tin roof."

Scarlet Tate gasped. "Well, I declare! Jackson Tate, you ain't got the good sense God gave ya."

Jackson leaned forward, "whispering" loudly, "Ya see what happens when you let a woman come to breakfast, boys?"

Nick saved his rib cage from another jab by reaching across the table, extending his hand. "I'm sorry, ma'am, but I never got your first name."

She shook. "Scarlet. And as you may have guessed, I'm married to this bozo."

Again, Jackson made an aside that wasn't an aside. "This is our dynamic. She calls me names, and I let her do it." He winked. "It's just easier that way."

"Jackson!" Scarlet thwapped him on the head, knocking his hat askew.

"Quit. Now you've gone and knocked my hat all cattywampus."

"You shouldn't be wearin' that hat in here anyways," she scolded. "Would you quit being so ugly. You'd think you were raised in a barn."

"Well, I was."

Daisy Mae Gardner sauntered up to the table, running her gaze over Nick, the hussy. "Hi, Nick." I bristled. Her tone was a tad too inviting for my liking. "Anyone want something sweet?" she asked, not taking her focus from Nick. No one could have missed her implied come-on.

Brooks slid me a look, clearing his throat. "Nah."

She glanced at him, and he rubbed his stomach.

"Stick a fork in me. I'm done."

She eyed Nick. "Maybe later then." She lingered on the "l" in later, before gathering some dirty plates and sashaying away, swinging her hips like she was aringin' a bell. We all watched her leave silently.

"You been messin' with that little girl?" I asked Nick sweetly.

"She wishes," Carter Beamer interjected.

I narrowed my gaze on the retreating figure. "I think I'll go and have me a talk with Miss Daisy."

I heard the men's low whistles as I marched away, and someone commented, I think it was that Beau fella, "Look out. Here comes a cat fight."

You've got that right.

"Be nice," Nick warned.

I spun, walking backwards as I said. "Oh, I will. But you remember this, sugar, Southern girls can bless hearts, but we can take names, too." I whirled and did a little hip shaking of my own as I strolled, following Daisy to the counter, ignoring the hoots and hubbub from the clan behind me.

"Is there somethin' I can help you with, Bobby Jo?" Daisy said icily.

"Why yes, Daisy, you can. Ya see, I ordered some sandwiches for Nick and me." I opened my stance to include the table, glancing their way. They were all listening in on the exchange with the interest that one finds in small towns for such things. "We're having us a picnic up at Bullock Overlook. Ya ever been there?" My dropping the name of a local make-out spot ruffled her fur, as I knew it would.

"Why do I feel like she just scored a point?" I heard Nick say.

"Because she did," Scarlet answered empathically.

"How nice for you," Daisy said with disdain. "I'll git those sandwiches for you."

She disappeared in the back, and I pivoted to the table and gave them the same little victory dance that Nick had earlier. But Daisy returned more quickly than I thought, and I had to change my gesture to swatting at the air. "Somebody let in a fly."

Her eyes were icicles. "Uh-huh. Here's your sandwiches." She dropped them onto the counter with a *thud*.

I was done playing with her, but I kept my act going. "Why, it must be exhausting being so unpleasant all the time."

She looked at me evenly then drew a breath. "It seems that someone didn't get enough hugs growing up." She smiled, knowing she'd hit a nerve. Everyone in town knew about my daddy's temper.

I snatched the bag. "Why, thank you, darling," I said, as sweet as pie. I half turned but spun again to face her. "Oh, I forgot to tip you when I called in my order. Here's my tip," I leaned in so that only she would hear me, "You stay away from Nick Adams. I've got enough dirt on you to dig a flower bed and landscape the whole town with it." With one more pointed glare I went back to my group, giving them a bow.

"Whooey!" Carter shouted. "I would have loved to have been a fly on the wall and caught that last shot you gave her."

"Well, I said something to the effects of, you try me, gal. 'Cause if I had my druthers, I'd knock you into next Sunday and save you a seat at church."

Everyone whooped it up at that one. Nick laughed. "Whoa. Remind me to never piss in your cereal." He was fitting right in. He leaned into the boys. "Y'all see my little badass?" he said, conjuring a Kentucky accent of his own. "She's sexy as hell." He drew Daisy's attention, swung me into a dip, sandwiches and all, and laid one on me. Our posse lost it.

"You ready to go?" he said in a low, husky tone, his eyes with a wicked gleam to them.

"I'll go anywhere with you, sweetheart."

The last thing I heard as I exited was Daisy, presumably talking to some customers seated at the counter, "I don't have the energy to hate her, but I sure don't like her."

Nick must have heard, too. "Ooh. I think you made yourself an enemy."

We looked through the window as we walked arm in arm past it. "Who her? I wouldn't trust her to babysit my pet rock."

He hugged me enthusiastically. "I believe I love this side of you."

"Quit. You're smashing our sandwiches."

He puckered his lips. "Come on, baby. Give me some sugar."

I laughed. We'd arrived at his car, so we parted, and he began to circle around to the driver's side.

"You better watch it, buddy. You're not off the hook yet. I'm still madder than the devil at a baptism."

"What? What'd I do?"

We got into the car. I crossed my arms. "You must have encouraged that little harlot in some way."

He held up his palms. "I swear, I didn't. You can ask the boys."

"Oh, it's the boys, now, is it? Well, I'm telling you, mister, you're one bad decision away from making it on the news." I was acting mad, but I also wasn't acting. In my heart I knew that Daisy Mae Gardner stood no chance with Nick. But that didn't mean a more sophisticated, smarter woman wouldn't turn his head. Daisy I could handle, but someone else...I wasn't so sure.

He began to leave his parking space, and some idiot increased his speed behind us so we couldn't go. "Y'all drive like bats out of hell around here," he commented, but then he had to concentrate on his driving.

It was about a half-hour drive to Kingdom Come State Park. He played some music, and we were singing along. "Foreigner," he said as one song started.

"What?"

"Oh. Sorry. Habit. Zoe and I used to like to call music. Like a contest, to see who got the name first."

"Oh. The song title?"

He glanced at me, surprised, I think, by my interest. "No. Only the artist." I watched him, a smile played on his lips.

"What?"

He looked at me. "Huh?"

"You were smiling."

"Oh. It's just...we were kind of obnoxious with it. We'd be in separate conversations, and we'd call a song in the middle of a sentence and then continue on." I stared at him. "Like...I'd be telling you a story and blurt out AC/DC in the middle of it, so I could beat Zoe to it, and then I'd continue on like nothing had happened. It was actually pretty rude, but we couldn't help it."

"Oh." I turned to peer through my window. I'd told him before that I didn't mind him talking about Zoe but coming this close to the Daisy episode, it bothered me. But it also made me sad for him. He'd lost both of his best friends. I twisted back, and he was smiling again. "What's so funny?"

He seemed apprehensive. My tone was sharper than I intended. "What?"

"You're smiling again."

"Am I? Oh." He nodded at the windshield. "Is this the entrance?"

He was being evasive. "You mean with the great big 'Welcome to Kingdom Come State Park' sign with the arrow? Yes, this is the entrance. Now tell me what's on your mind."

"Well..." I think he blushed. "It's kind of dumb, but Zoe and me—and Zack...her whole family, really—"

I waited impatiently for him to get to his point as we turned into the park.

"We used to...analyze music."

He had me curious. "What do you mean by analyze music?"

He peered out the windshield. "Wow. This is nice."

I looked around. "We haven't even really gotten into the park yet. What's nice?"

"Oh, you know...the trees." He was trying to change the subject.

"Nick, what do you mean by analyze music?"

He sighed. "Okay. Take that Foreigner song earlier, 'Hot Blooded'?"

"Yeah?"

"Well...there's a line in it that says something along the lines of having a fever of a hundred three degrees."

I nodded. "So?"

He steered the car into a parking spot and shut off the engine. "So, we'd say something stupid like, 'Lou Gramm, if you have a fever of one hundred three degrees, don't just sing about it. Take some ibuprofen.'"

My mouth hung open a little, and I stared at him. "And that's song analysis."

"Uhh...yeah. Like I said, it was stupid." He started to open his door and bail out of the car.

I had to smile. "You're right. It's stupid. But it's funny."

He shifted his weight back into the car. "You think so?"

I nodded. "It's clever."

He shrugged, but he looked a whole lot happier. "Yeah. I guess. Are you ready to hike?"

My lips lifted. "Let's do it."

But before he could leave, his phone buzzed. He pulled it from his pocket, peered at it with a frown, and put it away.

"Is it something you have to take care of?"

He grinned, tapping me on the nose. "Not today, I don't."

Five minutes into our hike, it vibrated again. He glanced at the display.

"Who is it?"

"Just Clint," he said dismissively. "He probably wants to tell me in vast and gory detail about his latest hunting trip."

Another five minutes passed when Nick griped, "Oh, for Pete's sake. What could be so all-fired important?"

"Maybe you should answer it."

"No. I'm on a hike in the beautiful outdoors with you," he grumbled.

The next time it rang, we were on the verge of breasting the top of the hill where I planned to picnic. It was a spot I knew of with a phenomenal view, but I was almost certain Nick would chuck his cell over the edge into the trees below if given the opportunity.

I sighed. "Clearly, he's not giving up."

He slid the button to answer, albeit somewhat violently. "This better be important, Clint," he growled, getting straight to the point. He listened, and his gaze widened. He swung so that his back was toward me, pacing away with his hand on his hip. "What the hell? Can we help it if we're burglarized?" He paused again, and I heard Clint yapping about something in an agitated manner. "Oh, for the love of Pete. That's ridiculous."

"I told you he's a loon," I could hear distinctly.

"All right. I'll take care of it." Nick looked at me and rolled his eyes. "I said I'll take care of it," he shouted. "I'm not sure. I'm in the middle of a hike, dammit. No. No!" He held the phone in front of him. "You're...cutting out. We must be...too high for reception." He made cracking noises in between his sentence fragments to mimic a bad connection, but I doubted Clint believed him. "I'll go a little higher...if I can get a better signal...if we get disconnected... call you...later. Is this bet—?" He ended the call but stood lost in thought for a moment.

"What's going on?"

He startled. "Oh...you know Clint. Panic is his go-to in any situation." He continued trekking up the hill. "He's gonna give himself an aneurysm," he mumbled.

A short while later, we broke from the trees into an open space not much bigger than our picnic blanket. "Holy cow," Nick exclaimed.

Before us spread rolling hills covered with dark green trees, sandwiched together to form a visual carpet over the valley below. Other than a few phone lines, the view was unbroken, making me wonder what it must have been like to be Lewis and Clark coming on vista after incredible, unsullied vista as they traveled west. The hills went on to the horizon, as far as we could see, rippling like ocean waves.

I stepped to Nick's side, and he put his arm around my shoulders. "I had no idea how amazing the view would be."

It was quiet, save the squawking of a hawk below us, and the rustle of the wind as it blew through the trees, disturbing their leaves. I felt a swelling of pride. In town, everything was ugly and coated with coal dust; but here, one could really appreciate the natural beauty of the state of my birth. Here I could call myself a Kentuckian with a sense of satisfaction.

We spread our blanket out and ate our sandwiches, along with some individual-sized bags of chips I'd picked up, and homemade chocolate chip cookies I'd stuck in the freezer a week ago.

"Damn these cookies are good," he said for the ninth time. "This isn't the standard recipe. What's in them?"

I shrugged. "Some cream cheese."

"Cream cheese...hmm."

I'd enjoyed lunch, but something was niggling at me. "So, what was Clint so upset about earlier?"

"Oh. You know we've got that Johnny Caine case..."

I nodded.

"Well, Mr. Caine said that he's suing us."

"*Suing* you? For what?"

A sly smile cracked his face. "Well, it seems you broke into my office."

I blinked. "Huh?"

"You broke into my office and stole Johnny Caine's file. Then you made public some very incriminating video footage."

I tilted my head, studying his face. He had to be messing with me. "Funny, because I don't remember breaking into your office."

"Oh, it was you, all right. Our Ring camera caught you. Your red suit and white cowboy hat were a dead giveaway."

What. The. Hell?

I felt sick to my stomach. "N-nick...I would never—"

He gripped my biceps. "I know. It wasn't you. It was someone attempting to frame you."

My head was still reeling. "How can you be certain it wasn't me then?"

"One, because you wouldn't do that. Two, because the perpetrator had fingernails painted like the American flag."

I gasped. "Michelle."

He nodded. "I think your boss was trying to kill two birds with one patriotic stone. Some sort of twisted revenge on me. And payback for you leaving the firm and not playing ball. Thank you for doing that, by the way."

I brushed that aside. "Oh, that was nothing. I can't believe—"

"That wasn't nothing. It was very brave and selfless."

Heat rose in my cheeks. "It was the right thing to do," I muttered.

"Yes. But most people would have chosen to save their own hides rather than jeopardize their job."

I barely heard him. "Nick, you have to go to Denver. They need you. This is your business we're talking about." I scrambled to my feet and gathered our picnic things. "You should never have come here to mess around with me."

He straightened his back. "Mess around?"

"Yes. Get off the blanket." I kicked him lightly.

He rose finally but instead of helping, he just stared at me.

I guess I'll pack everything up then. Thanks a lot.

"Let's go." I went to move past him, and he took my arm.

"We're not going anywhere," he snarled.

Surprised by his tone, I lifted my head.

"Did you think last night was about me 'messing around' with you?"

"Well...yeah."

He released me and spun his back to me, cocking a hip. "You thought you were another notch in my belt?"

Wasn't I?

I fought not to cry, not answering.

He was quiet, too. When he spoke, his voice was slow and low pitched. "Is that what last night was for you? It meant nothing?"

I wish it didn't mean anything. That I wasn't totally in love with you.

"I—" My voice was clogged with tears. I was glad he didn't turn.

Is he making me say it? That I love him. That I'll be crushed when he leaves.

But I'd never been one to back away from a fight.

I lifted my chin. "Last night was...everything for me. I'm an idiot for falling in love with you. I'm sorry. I didn't mean to, but it happened anyway. I'm sorry I've ruined everything, but I couldn't help it."

He exhaled.

I was losing it, and I wouldn't do it in front of him. "I'll just meet you at the car, okay? You can drop me off, then leave." I marched off at a quick pace, determined to escape from him, but he caught up with me and spun me around.

"Oh, Bobby Jo." He wiped my tears. "Last night..." He looked over my shoulder, as if his words were written there. "Last night was unlike anything I've ever experienced before."

My brow furrowed. What was he talking about?

He cupped my chin. "It was unlike anything I've ever experienced before because I've never...loved a woman as much as I love you." He moved his hands to my arms. "I thought I loved Zoe...I did love Zoe," he corrected. "But not in the way I love you. I didn't truly understand her, even though we'd been friends for forever. You and I...we haven't really known each other long, but...I may sound like an idiot saying this—and I hate sounding like an idiot—but...I feel like we belong together. Come back to Denver with me."

Is he saying this, or am I simply imagining it? Return to Denver with him? Was that even a possibility?

"But I have a business."

"Yeah." He sounded disappointed. As he walked around in a circle, his face brightened. "I'll move here."

Was he for real? "There's hardly enough work in this town for me. Two lawyers would be total overkill."

"Well, I'll find a different job. Surely, I can do more than just lawyering."

"Nick. You belong in the courtroom."

"Well, so do you," he countered. He exhaled. "There has to be a solution."

Did he really love me?

I was a little stunned by his revelation.

He snapped his fingers, startling me. "I've got it! There's no problem. We can keep your place here for when we need a getaway, or you want to come see your dad."

He wasn't being realistic. "I don't have a job in Denver."

"You'll come work with me."

"I don't know. You being my boss might not be a good—"

"I wouldn't be your boss. We'd be working together. Partners. I'll make you a partner."

"Oh, your other partners will love that. I waltz in as a partner?"

"It doesn't matter what they think. I'm senior partner. Plus, I think they'll be thrilled to have a lawyer of your caliber in our office."

I rolled my eyes. "Right."

He took my arms again. "Well, maybe thrilled is a little strong. But they'll get over it. Come back with me."

In the end, how could I say no. Especially when I didn't really want to.

CHAPTER TWENTY-SEVEN

N*ick*

It had been a month since our return to Denver, and things were going great. We split our time between her newly renovated place and mine but spent the majority of our time at The Randolph, since it was right across the street from the courthouse. I was at the courthouse chatting with a friend named Patrick Duggan while I waited outside a courtroom for Bobby Jo.

"Something's changed about you, Nick," he said.

But I was barely paying attention as people had begun to file out of the door behind him. "You think so?"

"Yeah. You seem...happy. Less angry. Nicer, even."

Little did he know that the reason for those changes was strutting toward me wearing a white suit that was making my heart beat faster. It was funny since another acquaintance had mentioned earlier, unaware of our relationship, that the "Cold-hearted Temptress of the Courthouse" seemed to have thawed some. I liked to think that her change had been inspired by me. She smiled more and was more comfortable letting her guard down around people, showing them the incredible woman that hid beneath that icy façade.

"Hey, handsome," she purred, giving me a kiss that I would have loved to take deeper, had Patrick not been standing there.

"Oh," he said, grinning. "Now I get it."

I was introducing her when a gunshot rang through the building. We were not far from the atrium where we could see the gunman with a pistol raised to the ceiling. We ducked for cover around the corner of a hall that intersected with the one we'd been on.

"Where is B.J. McCaffrey?" the lunatic raved.

"Oh, shit," she moaned.

"You recognize this guy?"

She nodded, her face pale. "I represented his wife. You remember, the abusive guy from Texas..."

She'd told me of the case and how relieved she was when the judge sided with her in keeping his two young daughters away from the violent man.

"B.J...." he bellowed. "I know you can hear me. Get that sexy little ass of yours out here. I'm madder than three shades of hell, and you're the reason for it."

I knew the determined look in Bobby Jo's eyes and so wasn't surprised when she made a move to confront him. I yanked her behind the cover of the wall.

"What the hell do you think you're doing?" I hissed.

"Nick, it's me he wants. Someone could get hurt."

"Yeah," I said indignantly. "You." Over her shoulder I saw a janitor leaving a closet, presumably heading for the hills. "I'm sorry," I said.

Her cute little brow furrowed. "For what?"

"For this." I grabbed her and dragged her back a few feet, shoving her through the open closet door and shutting it in her face.

"Nick Adams!" she yelled as I put my weight against the door she was beating on. "You better let me out of here. I'm mad enough to chew up a broom stick and spit toothpicks."

I loved it when her Harlan emerged. But at the moment, I had other things to worry about. I looked at Patrick. "Come over here and help me." Being the obliging man that he was, he came to lean against the door with me. "Now keep her in there."

Pressing against the wall, I inched toward the corner to get a peek at the shooter.

"If you don't show, I'm gonna pick off people one at a time. Startin' with the gal hidin' behind the sandwich cart."

Someone yelped.

I took a deep breath and rounded the corner with my hands in the air.

He shoved some teenaged girl in a Meat Me in the Atrium T-shirt away from him, and she scrambled off. He trained his .45, or whatever it was, on me.

"Easy. Easy. I just want to talk to you." I advanced slowly, stopping while still some distance from him. I didn't want him to feel threatened.

He spit to the side. "Who the hell are you?"

"Nick Adams. Nice to meet you," I said dryly. I could see the unarmed security guards sneaking up behind him. I needed to keep him occupied so they could jump him.

"I wish I could say the same. Now you either tell me where B.J. McCaffrey is, or you can skip your happy ass on out of here."

"Listen...what is your name again?"

"Carl."

"Listen, Carl. You don't want to shoot anyone."

"The hell I don't. And you seem to be volunteering, so..."

The next thing I knew, there was an explosion and searing pain ripped through me. The guards tackled him and wrestled the gun from his hand as I staggered backward, hitting the wall and sliding down.

"Nick!" Bobby Jo yelled. She came running to me, her eyes wide and wild, Patrick chasing after her. She fell to her knees beside me. "Oh, my God. He shot you."

I tried to focus on her as things were getting bleary. "Yes. I know, darling."

"You're bleeding."

A fact I also knew.

"Oh, my God," she sobbed. "What should I do?" Blood was all over her suit.

She looked so pathetic. I went to lift my arm to touch her face and comfort her, but a scream burst from my lips.

"Fuck that hurts." I slid down more, suddenly struggling to hold my head up.

"Nick. Nick!" she shrieked. Her voice was muffled by the fog surrounding me. Then everything went black.

When I woke after surgery, Bobby Jo was standing, trembling, by my bedside, appearing to be as likely to fall apart as that crooked door on her daddy's front porch.

"Oh, Nick! Nick," she cried, leaning over the rail so that she could brush the hair from my face. "I'm so sorry."

Why? Did you shoot me?

I was a little unclear at first, but I remembered bit by bit. I was so tired. I closed my eyes but croaked out, "You're okay?"

She laughed through her tears for some reason. "I'm fine. You're the one who got shot."

"So that really did happen," I mumbled.

"Shh. Just rest now, honey."

I faded off. When I woke again, a doctor was explaining to Bobby Jo that the shot entered my shoulder and exited my back but didn't hit "anything important."

I beg to differ. It hit me, after all.

"Ahh. There he is. How are you feeling, Mr. Adams?"

"Like shit, Doc. How are you?"

He chuckled. "I see you haven't lost your sense of humor. That's good."

He proceeded to put me through a bunch of agonizing maneuvers but, sadistically, seemed glad at my responses. "You'll be just fine, Mr. Adams," he told me. "In a couple of months, you should be good as new."

"Except for the holes in me," I said wryly.

He didn't get it. "Oh, yes. I'm afraid there will be a few scars, but they should be fairly small."

"Great." I could feel myself drifting away again. "Bobby Jo?"

"Yes, honey. I'm here. What do you need?"

I forced my eyes open. "Nothing. I wanted to see your face."

She took my hand, clutching it in both of hers and raising it to her lips. "I was so scared, Nick."

"I know," I said softly. "But you heard the doc, I'm fine."

"Thank the Lord. Why did you do that?"

Her tears dripped onto me. "I'm not sure." I went to shrug and moaned.

"Does it hurt? Doctor, I think he's in pain."

He studied me. "You doing all right, Mr. Adams?"

I nodded, but I must have fallen asleep, because I don't remember anything else.

It was a month after I'd been shot, and we were meeting Zoe and Zack for dinner at a new place called Under Arrest, a block from The Randolph. It was below ground level, thus the under, and all of the new places in the vicinity were copying Unwarranted in pandering to the courthouse crowd, including a spot called The Trial Bar. I was anxious to see my friends as it had been quite a while. We'd made plans a couple of times, then things would come up, and one of us would have to cancel. I was excited to introduce them to Bobby Jo.

"You can call me B.J.," she said right away. "*He* can't," she said, jerking her thumb at me, "but you can."

I had been surprised by Zoe's baby bump, but even more shocked when the fact that she was carrying Zack's child didn't bother me as much as I thought it would.

"So, how are you doing, Nickie?"

"Bet your jump shot sucks," Zack joked.

"Yeah, but I still could beat you."

"Boys. Boys!" Zoe chided. "They're a pair of morons," Zoe told Bobby Jo.

"Clearly," she returned with a wink.

"Hey. Hey. Don't you two gang up on me," I protested, but I squeezed her hand on the table. I saw Zoe take in a breath and elbow Zack.

The girls both had a version of a lemon drop martini in front of them. The establishment had again stuck to the legal theme in titling it an Appeeling Martini. I had gone for an especially dry V Is for Verdict Vodka Martini, and Zack ordered an Arbitration Ale.

He leaned forward. "So, tell us about this harrowing experience at the courthouse."

"Well," I said, taking a moment to recall the incident. "It started out like a normal day."

Bobby Jo nodded.

"Then some loon came into the lobby and shot off a gun."

"He was a former client of yours, wasn't he?" Zoe asked her.

"Yes."

"He was screaming her name... You tell it."

"He was yelling for me. I'd represented his wife in a divorce case and was partly responsible for having his children taken away from him."

Zoe and Zack nodded, following the story but exchanging a look.

"They needed to be removed from his custody," Bobby Jo reassured him. "He was a violent man."

I lifted my sling. "As you can see."

"So, how did you get involved?" Zoe asked.

"Well," I eyed Bobby Jo. "She was going out there to confront him."

"He was after me. There was no reason for anyone else to get hurt."

Zoe and Zack shifted their gazes between Bobby Jo and me.

"No way in hell would I let that happen..."

"So, he shoved me into a janitor's closet," she crossed her arms, glaring at me. "And had his friend keep me there."

"You were being unreasonable," I said to defend myself.

"*I* was being unreasonable?" she squawked.

Zack interrupted our squabble. "What happened next?"

"Well...I tried to talk to the guy. He didn't like what I was saying, I guess, and he shot me."

"It was awful," Bobby Jo added, staring at the table.

"Change the subject," I mouthed to Zack.

"So, where are you from, B.J.?" He looked at me smugly, owning his right to call her that. "I thought I detected a slight accent."

"Harlan, Kentucky."

"Ahh. What brought you to the legal field?"

"I don't know. I've always been good at arguing."

"That's for damned sure," I joked.

"Hey." My teasing helped to lighten the mood.

A few minutes later, she leaned into me. "Journey."

"Good call."

"Wait. Did she just call the song?" Zoe asked. She tilted her head with a smile. "Game on."

We all called songs for the rest of the evening, with a fairly equal score between the four of us.

At one point, Bobby Jo spun her martini glass by the stem, a wicked gleam in her eye. "Have you guys ever been to Unwarranted?"

They both nodded.

"We've met Nick there a few times for drinks," Zack supplied.

"Did Nick ever tell you about the time he drank his way through the entire Felonies list on their menu?"

"You're kidding me. Those are 'legally lethal'. You didn't drive home after that, did you?"

I smirked, and she squirmed, knowing that he'd given me the advantage. I intentionally twirled my glass as B.J. had, drawing the moment out. "That was the first night that Bobby Jo took me to her place." I wiggled my brows.

"Stop." She punched my arm, her face flushed.

"Ouch."

She lifted her chin. "Oh, don't be such a baby."

I rubbed it then dropped it over her shoulder, pulling her into my side.

She sipped her martini, focusing on me, and suddenly I was the one sweating. I loved our conversational sparring...which invoked the idea of parrying and thrusting, and my thoughts went off rail. She ran a painted fingernail along my jaw; I zeroed in on the way her lips were moving. "I only escorted him up to my place..." She had her audience in her hand; we were all holding our breath, waiting for the other shoe to drop. "...to save him from being arrested."

"Arrested?" Zack and Zoe said at the same time, their gazes widening.

I shrugged. "I got into a fight."

"Did you win?" Zack countered.

"What do you think, genius?"

Bobby Jo sat back, looking smug and enjoying her little victory.

"Oh, I like her, Nickie," Zoe said, a twinkle in her eye. "She gives you as much shit as we do."

They regaled her with stories of the old Nick. Or what I liked to think of as the old Nick.

After Zoe told a particularly unflattering story, Bobby Jo commented, "Wow. He really was an asshole, wasn't he?"

"Come on, guys. I've got the gal to like me. I don't want her to hear about all the old shit I used to do."

"Don't worry. You were kind of a jerk when we first got together, too." She put a hand to her mouth as if shielding it to talk to Zoe. "Completely self-absorbed."

Zoe nodded knowingly.

"But I love you anyway."

"Gee, thanks."

Zoe's eyes lit up with her mention of the L-word.

I changed the subject and gave them a colorful description of the Poke Sallet Festival, which they enjoyed immensely.

We had a great dinner, dessert, after-dinner drinks... The crowd was thinning out when Bobby Jo excused herself to go to the bathroom. But I knew she was doing it to torture me with the way she moved in the emerald green, silky little number she was wearing that she knew always got me going. The manner in which the fabric hugged her hips ought to have been illegal. I ran my gaze along her. She flipped her hair as she cast a smoldering look over her shoulder.

Zoe rose and slid into the booth with me, bouncing to my side.

"Easy, Zoe. I'm still in a sling."

She ignored me. "Holy shit, Nick! You're in love with her." She meant to embarrass me.

I focused on B.J. again as she shimmied across the floor, disappearing behind the restroom door. I sighed. "Head over heels."

She hugged my arm painfully and shrieked. "I can't believe it! Nick Adams has fallen!"

Zack sat back. "She's great, Nick. Intelligent, witty...she's gonna give you a run for your money."

"Oh..." I chuckled. "I ain't running."

Zoe noogied me. "Our little Nickie is growing up."

I swatted at her. "Knock it off."

She squeezed me tighter. "She's awesome. She really is." Zoe suddenly switched from torturer to sobbing mess. "I'm so happy for you."

I looked at Zack with wide eyes.

"Hormones."

"I thought I saw something. You guys are having a kid?"

Zack beamed, and Zoe nodded, splashing me with tears.

I offered Zack my hand. "Congratulations, man."

Zoe grabbed me, laying her cheek on my chest. "Everything is going well for all of us."

"Yeah, about eight years too late," I said, chagrined.

She separated and peered into my face. "No. It's how it was supposed to be."

Zack bobbed his head. "Maybe we just weren't ready for it yet back then."

I lifted my gaze. Bobby Jo was standing near the table with her arms folded. "I leave for two seconds, and you're all over her," she said cooly. She twisted on her heels to rush away.

"No, wait," I shouted, alarmed. "Move, Zo," I sniped as she tried to scoot her pregnant ass out of my way. "Bobby Jo, let me explain."

She stopped. Her shoulders were shaking.

"Babe, it's not what it seems like." I spun her and realized she wasn't crying; she was laughing her ass off. "You little shit!"

She was bent in half, laughing so hard she had to lay her hand on the table to retain her balance. Zack and Zoe joined in. I was surprised by how at ease she seemed around them. The alcohol must have relaxed her. Plus, they all seemed to get along so well. I pulled Bobby Jo into my arms but whacked her tush. "No more martinis for you. You're getting unmanageable."

She pursed her lips. "I'm sorry, baby." She cooed. "I just couldn't resist."

"Whatever," I grumbled, but I was amused by her behavior.

She played with the hair at the back of my neck, and it was suddenly like Zack and Zoe didn't exist. "Let me make it up to you." She lowered her mouth to mine with a kiss that set me on fire.

Zack and Zoe oohed and ahhed like a couple of high schoolers.

I jerked my head in their direction. "Let's lose these two so I can peel this dress off you and punish you properly," I growled.

"Ooh," she squealed, grabbing her purse.

We said our goodbyes and left.

CHAPTER TWENTY-EIGHT

N*ick*

A few months later, it was my turn to cook. Once my wound had begun to heal, we'd made a rotation. I would make the shopping list the night prior, and she would purchase what we needed at the market inside The Randolph while I changed and got ready to cook. When I got to her condo, however, the door was ajar. I stepped inside, but when I went to close the door, it wouldn't latch.

"What the hell? They just put this in." I messed with it a little, but it seemed like it was jacked up. "Honey? Did you know your door is broken?"

I paused, listening. There was no reply. That's when I got the first inkling that something was amiss. She shouldn't have even been home yet. She'd left the office before me, but I'd given her a pretty extensive shopping list.

I wonder if she wasn't feeling well and came home.

"Honey?" I ventured into the condo further. Nothing seemed out of place. "Bobby Jo?" I opened the door to her bedroom and swung it wide. Nothing. Nobody. I attributed it to an overactive imagination and spun to walk down the hall. I felt movement and whirled.

I gasped. Water dripped into my eyes. I blinked to clear them and found Greg Zonderbond sitting on the edge of Bobby Jo's coffee table, holding a half empty glass. I jerked forward but couldn't rise. My hands were bound, as were my feet. My head weighed too much for me to lift it, and I couldn't think through blinding pain. My shoulder, where I'd been shot, screamed.

"Greg?"

He set the glass behind him. "Nick Adams. I've been waiting a long time for this."

This? What was this?

He drew himself slowly to his feet, then, like lightning, pounded his fist into my jaw. My neck strained in its effort to keep my head attached, and blood spurted from my mouth and nose onto B.J.'s white carpeting.

She'll kill me.

Greg was...was he crying? "You son of a bitch!" He wiped his nose with the back of his hand as I tried to drag air into my aching chest. It wasn't the first hit I'd taken, but I didn't remember the others. "You didn't even give a shit about her."

"Who?" I mumbled, my lips swollen and cracked, blood filling my throat. "Sarah?" I coughed and couldn't see the uppercut that hit me.

"Don't you say her name, you bastard!"

What is going on?

The door thudded against the chain he must have latched.

B.J.!

"Nick? Why do you have the chain on the door? Is this lock broken?"

I opened my mouth to warn her, but Greg yanked a bandana up from my chest to gag me. He snatched a gun that had been hidden behind him on the coffee table and slipped into the kitchen so that he could come at the door from the blind side.

"Nick? What's going on?"

I contorted my neck to watch him as he pushed the door closed, almost smashing her in it.

"Hey! Careful."

He silently slid the chain from the latch and let it swing loose.

"No!" I screamed, but only a muffled noise could be heard.

"Nick, why is this—?" She walked through the door, toting a bag of groceries, and saw me. "Nick! Oh, my God."

I shook my head, trying to warn her, but as she moved toward me, he grabbed her hair, jerking her back. She dropped the groceries, and he kicked them clear of his path as he dragged her forward. "Oh!" She tried to pry his fingers free, but he knocked her knees out from under her, sending her tumbling down the steps, crashing into the side of the chair I was strapped to, leaving his fist full of hair. She immediately spun and sat, ready to defend herself, but his blow still caught her hard across the mouth, and she screamed. He crouched, cocked his gun, and held it to her temple.

"You make another sound like that, I'll kill you. Got it, Barbara Jean?"

She nodded, and I could see she was shaking.

"Leave her alone!"

I guess my garbled words were intelligible as he said, "What? You don't like me touching your girl? Well, you'll see a whole lot more than that. Get up, B.J."

She hesitated.

"Get on your feet!" he railed.

She stood, and he grabbed her, shoving her toward the couch. He was out of his mind. The door was still partially open. Anyone could walk by and hear him.

"Now, Barbara Jean..." He turned to sneer at me. "Take off your clothes."

"Wh-hat?"

"You heard me, take off your clothes."

"I'm not taking—"

"Oh, you want me to help." He slammed the gun on the table, took hold of her shirt, and ripped it open as he pushed her onto the couch.

I went nuts, cursing, lunging and straining, moving the chair closer to them with my struggles. He was on top of her, trapping her arms above her head as she thrashed, trying to unseat him.

"Oh, wait." He stilled, looked at me, and released her. Straightening, he took his weight from her and snatched his gun from the table. "Our friend has something to say to us. Let's see what that is."

He came and ripped the bandana away from my mouth. "What the hell is wrong with you?" I panted. "You got Sarah in the end. Why do you hate me so much?"

"I got Sarah in the end," he repeated, running his tongue along his teeth. "Yeah, that's what I thought, too. Until I walked into our bedroom and found her pleasuring herself while watching videos of the two of you screwing." He was livid, the veins pulsing in his neck.

"The two of us...?" What was he *talking about*? "You mean in college?"

"You don't even remember. That's how little you cared for her. But I loved her, man." His voice broke. "I loved her, and she loved *you*. And now neither of us will have her because she's dead."

I blinked, and a chill washed over me. "Sarah's dead?"

"I told you not to say her name." He jabbed me again in the face, toppling my chair. My head bounced off the floor on impact.

"Nick!" Bobby Jo sobbed.

Zonderbond kicked me in the mouth.

"Stop!" Bobby Jo cried. "Please, stop."

He turned on her. "Why do you still have clothes on? I told you to undress."

I spit out blood. "She's not undressing for you, you son of a bitch."

He kicked me again, this time in the gut. I winced and sucked in air.

"Nick!" B.J. shrieked. "Stop! Stop! I'll do what you want. Just leave him alone."

Zonderbond grinned at me, jerking my chair upright. “Now we'll have some fun.” He swung back to her.

She shrugged free of her ripped shirt.

Tears came to my eyes. I couldn't help her, couldn't prevent him from hurting her, and it was killing me. “You sick bastard. Don't touch her.”

“Nick. It's all right.” Something in the way she said it, and how she looked at me, told me she had a plan.

“Listen to her, Adams. She's smart as well as beautiful.” With the last he seized her arms and pulled her against his body. “Aren't you, B.J.?” He ran his hand along her side.

“I'll kill you. I'll fucking kill you!” I shouted.

He twisted to taunt me. “Oh? And how are you doing that? Huh? You're not. You'll watch me—”

Bobby Jo took advantage of his momentary distraction and grabbed her half-melted welding helmet from the coffee table. We hadn't gotten a stand for it yet. When he turned back to her, she swung it with all her might, clobbering him on the side of his head. He went down in an instant. She stared at his body for a moment then rushed to me. “Oh, your poor face,” she cried, tenderly cupping my chin and examining it with tears in her eyes.

“I'm all right.” I smiled—though it was painful—to reassure her. “Get the gun.”

She retrieved it and was walking to me, but I stopped her.

“Do you have something that can cut these ropes?”

She disappeared into the kitchen for a minute then returned. It was difficult for her to get through the tough rope, and the more she worked on it, the more it bit into my skin. I gritted my teeth. When it finally dropped away, the blood rushing to my hands burned, but I threw my arms around her. I was so overcome with emotion, I couldn't talk at first. I drew back, bookending her face.

“Are you all right?”

She nodded rapidly, but he'd hurt her, split her lip, torn her hair out, and, I would discover later, left a deep bruise on her abdomen where the stair hit her.

"Okay. Give me the gun and call the cops before he wakes up."

She started to give it to me then stopped. "Do you know how to shoot?"

"Good point. I'll call the cops."

Greg was arrested, but that didn't keep him from my dreams or Bobby Jo's. The cuts and bruises might have healed, but we would never forget what we'd been through together, and what could have happened. But we tried our hardest to put it behind us and return to our normal life.

During the next several months, we began to hang out with Zack and Zoe on a regular basis. We would meet for drinks or play cards at one of our places. Bobby Jo and I invited them to her condo for a fabulous gourmet dinner that I had absolutely nothing to do with, other than opening the wine. We attempted a little two-on-two basketball at the court near their condo, but Bobby Jo had never played before. The next week, as was par for the course, she watched videos and read about basketball. She made me play every night after work until she became halfway decent at the sport.

Working together was going along well, too. We were in the conference room one day, preparing for a trial, when I glanced up because Bobby Jo hadn't answered my question. Her face had drained, and she was staring over my shoulder at the door. Alarmed, I swiveled in my chair. My jaw dropped, too.

She finally found her voice. "Daddy?" She rose. "What are you doing here?"

"I've come for a visit," he said simply.

She strode toward him. "But...you've never come for a visit before. In fact, to my knowledge, you've never left Harlan before." I got to my feet and followed.

"All the more reason," he countered. "I wanted to see what my little girl does."

She smiled. "You look nice."

He was wearing a suit. It was wrinkled and threadbare, but it was a suit.

He spun the fedora he held by the rim. "Well, I wouldn't want to embarrass you."

"Daddy, I would never be embarrassed by you," she answered immediately, totally sincere.

He stared at her and blinked for a moment, then shifted his gaze to the room. "So, this is where you work?"

"This is where Nick and I work. You remember Nick, don't you, Daddy?"

He eyed me briefly then extended his hand. "Yes. How are you doing?"

I shook, still a bit baffled by his showing up out of the blue. "Uhh...fine. And you?"

He glanced down. "It's going good. Going good," he repeated. Then, apparently at a loss for words, he added, "Well, I wouldn't want to keep y'all."

"Oh, no, Daddy. It's fine. I can show you around, and then we can take you to lunch. Are you staying long?"

He tilted his chin, still staring at the carpeting and shuffling his feet. "Uhh...I'm not sure..."

"Do you have a hotel?"

He lifted his head, becoming more animated. "Yes. But they're way more expensive here than in Harlan. Were you aware of that?"

"Yes. But I can help you with that."

"I don't 'cept no charity. You know that, Bobby Jo," he said gruffly.

"Oh, of course. It's only...I have some free points that I could use."

His brow furrowed. "Free points?"

"Yes. When you stay at hotels, they give you points for your next stay. When you have enough points, you can use them for a free night."

"Is that right? Huh." He stared at Bobby Jo. "What's wrong?"

She'd become teary-eyed. "Nothin'," she said, her Kentucky drawn out by his nearness. "I'm just...surprised to see you, is all. Is there another reason you came to Denver?"

"I came to see you. Ain't a daddy allowed to—" He began hacking, pulling a blue bandana from the rear pocket of his suit and holding it over his mouth.

"Are you okay? Do you want some water?"

I stepped up. "I can get some water."

"No. No." He waved his hand. "I'll be fine in a minute." He did get his coughing under control, but I was alarmed when I thought I saw blood on his bandana. "Ya know. I think I'll just go back to the hotel and lie down for a minute or two. Thank you for the lunch offer, though."

"Dinner then?" Bobby Jo asked eagerly. "We have to celebrate your visit. Our treat." He was about to protest, but she waved her arm. "You fed me half my life. I can buy you one meal."

"Yeah, but I didn't feed you well," he said softly.

"I ate fine," she responded, although her voice trembled.

"Can a beans ain't fine, Bobby Jo."

"It's fine enough. It prepared me for law school," she grinned, trying to make a joke of it.

He frowned. "I didn't help with that neither."

"That's all right. I didn't need help."

This made him smile for some reason. "Nah. You never did." He looked at me. "My little girl is tougher than all of us."

I nodded. "She is. She scares the shit out of me sometimes."

He laughed. "She should. She knows how to take care of herself."

I grabbed her hand and squeezed it. "She sure does."

He started coughing again but quickly fought it off. "I think I'll just go back to my hotel now. But I'll take you up on that dinner. I'll meet you at that fancy-assed condo of yours, and you can show me the place. What time?"

She peered at me. "Five-thirty?"

"That should work."

He nodded sharply. "Five-thirty it is." He turned and stepped into the hall but spun. "I'm proud of you, Bobby Jo." He hurried away.

She stood with one arm wrapped around her middle, covering her mouth as tears streamed down her face. I'm sure it was something that she dreamed of hearing for a long time.

"Are you all right?"

She said she was, but I drew her into my embrace anyway and kissed her hair. "It's all right, babe. If you need to cry, then you just cry."

Luckily, she had composed herself by the time my partner, Sheri Drew, came in. Sheri was an immigration lawyer. She stuck her head into the conference room where we had settled into our work again, files spread all across the table. "Sorry it took a while for me to get back from lunch. Some old man collapsed on the sidewalk out front, and I had to wade past the crowd to get to the door."

A sick feeling washed through me. I rose slowly and went to the window, watching as the paramedics pulled the sheet over his face. I squeezed my eyes shut.

"That's awful," Bobby Jo murmured. "Poor man. Do you think it was a heart attack? He didn't jump, did he?" she added hurriedly.

"I'm not sure," Sheri said thoughtfully. "It was weird. Blood was everywhere. It made me sick. But...he didn't seem...like, damaged. I would just expect a body to look worse if it fell from a height."

I think Bobby Jo realized what had happened then. I heard it in her voice. "Nick? What are you—"

I turned to her, and she read it in my face.

"No." She shook her head as if she could will it away. "Not now. Not now," she said the last as if begging, and the tears fell.

"What?" Sheri asked, she glanced from her to me. "Did you know him?"

We didn't answer. I walked toward Bobby Jo, and she came to me. I held her as her heart broke.

Her father must have recognized somehow that the end was near. That's why he came. He needed her to understand that he loved her and was proud of her.

I never felt so helpless in my life.

CHAPTER TWENTY-NINE

Nick

We were at Zoe and Zack's, on the balcony. Zoe had asked for Bobby Jo's help with the meal. Cooking wasn't one of her talents.

Zack and I followed them with our gazes as they crossed to the kitchen. "How's she doing?" They'd been kind enough to come to the services for Bobby Jo's father a month ago.

I shrugged. "It's hard to tell..." I thought over the past year. "I guess pretty good for a girl who's been attacked in her condo, had it set on fire, had a boyfriend treat her like trash, had an ex-client shoot aforementioned boyfriend, had an ex-boss attack her and said boyfriend, and had her father die on the doorstep of her building, minutes after expressing his love for her for the first time."

"Yeah," Zack said slowly. "That's a lot to handle. I'm surprised she's standing."

"Me, too." I took a drink from my tumbler and leaned on the balcony railing, staring out at the city. "I don't know, man. I'd like to do something for her that would sort of distract her from all the stuff that's been going on, but I can't think of anything good enough."

His face brightened. "Well, an old, wise teacher once said—"

I smirked. "Let me guess...you."

"Maybe...anyway, an old, wise teacher once said, when choosing a gift for a girl—or a distraction, like you said—it has to be tailored to her needs-slash-wants-slash-desires."

"Are you giving me dating advice? I never thought I'd see the day. It wasn't long ago you wanted to throw me off this balcony."

"That's in the past. As Zoe says—"

"We're beginning a new page," we both said at once.

We chuckled but lifted our heads when the slider squeaked open.

"So..." Zoe and Bobby Jo exchanged a look. Both of them seemed to be suppressing laughter. "How would you guys feel about eating at The Irish Snug?"

Zack faked a frown. "What did you do?"

She grimaced. "I may have skipped a line in the recipe?"

"Such as?"

"Such as, I was supposed to sear the chicken before putting it into the crockpot." She glanced at Bobby Jo. "And...turn the crockpot on."

Zack rolled his eyes. "Oh, boy. Well, come on. Get your coat."

Zoe clapped. "Goody."

They went inside, and we followed. I put my hand on the small of Bobby Jo's back. "Did she ruin dinner on purpose?"

The corners of her lips twitched. "I'll never tell."

We had a nice evening, and as I was about to drift off to sleep that night, I came up with an idea.

The next morning, Bobby Jo and I played a little tennis, which was definitely her sport. She absolutely obliterated me. From there we went to the animal shelter, which was our custom. She'd fallen in love with a long-haired German Shepherd, who was an absolutely adorable fur ball, and I'd decided to get him for her as the distraction.

Unfortunately, when we got to the shelter, his cage was empty with a sign on it saying he'd found his "furever home." It was another blow for Bobby Jo. I opted to take her to my mom's after that, again hoping for a distraction, and the visit went well, despite Mom calling Bobby Jo Zoe twice.

A week later I got a call.

"Hey, Nick. This is Julie from Denver Animal Shelter."

"Yes?"

What would she be calling for?

"You know that German Shepherd mix that B.J. was so fond of?"

"Uh-huh."

"The new owner brought him back. He got promoted and has to move to New York and doesn't want to take the pup there."

Bobby Jo was in the shower, but I still whispered. "You're an angel, Julie. Could you do me a favor?"

I hurriedly finished our conversation.

When Bobby Jo walked in, I was beaming.

She eyed me. "What's up with you?"

"Wanna go to the shelter?"

She was wearing a towel and brushing her hair. "Oh, honey. I don't know. I don't really feel like it."

I hugged her from behind, looking at her in the mirror. "What if I told you that German Shepherd mix is back?"

Her face brightened. "What? Why? How do you know?"

"Julie called me. The owner is moving to New York and doesn't want to take him."

She squealed. "Let's go."

When we got there, however, she was devastated to see his cage empty.

"Oh, he's gone already."

"Oh?" I said merrily. She spun, to chew me out, I think, but I said, "Look at the new owner."

She twisted back to read my name and whirled around. Julie was letting the little beast in the door. As soon as he saw Bobby Jo, he skirted me and ran to her, knocking her over in his exuberance and licking her to death.

He proved to be an excellent distraction and helper.

A week later, we were having breakfast on the balcony at her place, she in a nightgown and robe, I in a T-shirt and pajama pants. It was a perfect spring day, the sun shining and not a cloud in the sky. A simple breakfast of bacon and eggs was set before us, along with these wickedly good cranberry muffins that she'd made.

After a few minutes, I went in to "get more orange juice" and returned, setting Harlan, Bobby Jo's dog, on the floor behind her. Of course, he ran and jumped on her lap. We'd taken two dogs home that day as I couldn't take the pathetic, lost stare of this tiny terrier mix, white with a black eye patch. He looked so sad, I couldn't stand it. I named him Objection, thinking it would be funny to yell it out when I called him.

She set the paper aside. "Oh, you scamp. What are you up to?" She rubbed her face on his head. "What do you have on?"

I sat opposite her and snagged the paper, pretending to read it.

"Nick? Did you put this leather pouch on Harlan's neck?"

I smiled and put the paper down. "Leather pouch? Whatever are you talking about?"

She narrowed her gaze on me. "This leather pouch. Is it to hold the doggie poop bags?"

I shrugged. "I don't know. Maybe you should open it."

She stared at me for a moment more, trying to get a read on me then snapped it open and withdrew a piece of paper. "What is this?"

Instead of answering her, I called my dog. "Objection. Come here, boy."

She unfolded the page and read.

"I've been summoned?" She grinned, enjoying my little game. "What crime have I committed?"

"Witchcraft."

"Witchcraft? That would be covered under freedom of religion, counselor. Besides, what kind of witchcraft have I employed? Where's your evidence?"

I lifted my hand to indicate her dog. "Exhibit A."

"Harlan?"

"Yes." I rose. "If it pleases the court, I have several character witnesses..." I waved Zack and Zoe in. "...that will testify that I had no intention of having a dog."

Bobby Jo straightened as our friends entered, gawking at them. I pulled a chair out. "Mrs. Issaacs, if you'd please take the stand."

Zoe had a seat. I hadn't told them what I was up to, so she was as curious as Bobby Jo.

"Now, Mrs. Issaacs, do you recall an incident in the spring of our freshman year involving a dog?"

Zoe's eyes sparkled with laughter. "Do I ever? We were playing football on Zack's front lawn. Nick missed my pass and—"

"It was overthrown by a mile," I couldn't help but interject. It was an ongoing argument.

"It was not."

I put a hand on my hip. "Yes, it was, and you know it."

"Maybe if you'd just—"

Zack cleared his throat loudly, which got me back on track. "What happened next, Mrs. Issaacs, in your own words?"

She glared at me. "*In my own words,* Nick missed the pass..." She rushed past that before I could correct her. "...and it sailed over his head into Old Man Webster's yard. Old Man Webster did *not* like kids."

"He was scary," Zack added.

"And even scarier was his dog. A half-deaf, half-blind poodle/Shih Tsu mix that always looked disheveled. Anyway, Nick went to get the ball, because, clearly, he knew it was his fault that it wasn't caught..."

"Zoe," I warned.

"And he returned—"

Here she and Zack lost it.

Zoe was holding her stomach as she rocked, laughing her little head off. "It was so funny. Nick came running, and Charlie—that was the name of Old Man Webster's dog—was—" She busted out again. "It was the funniest thing I've ever seen in my life."

"Zoe!"

"Charlie was hanging from Nick's jeans like a football flag."

And, of course, Zack had to have his say. "And Old Man Webster's yelling," Zack tried to imitate his neighbor, "'You better bring my dog back here, boy, or I'll send your soul to Jesus and let Him deal with it.'"

I crossed my arms, leaning against the balcony railing, waiting for them to settle down. Bobby Jo was laughing as hard as they were.

Zoe wheezed a little. "Oh, my side hurts."

"I have one more question. If you think you can control your outbursts."

"I don't know," she looked at the other two, "but I'll try."

"In your earlier testimony you mentioned that my ass was bit by Charlie." There was a ripple of laughter, which I squashed with a glare. "What did I say after that about dogs?"

Zoe took a spoon from the table and used it as a microphone. "You said you'd never own a dog in your life."

"Exactly. Now get out of that seat," I said, yanking her onto her feet.

"Oh, I'm dismissed?" she said innocently.

"Yes," I scowled, "you're dismissed."

I turned to Bobby Jo, then I whirled around. "One more thing...jury instructions. From here on, you're not to say a word. Got it?"

Zack bowed his head and scooted back. "Got it."

"Zoe?"

"Hmm? Oh, got it."

"Now," I grasped my wrist behind me and paced, as I often did at trial. "Ladies and gentleman of the jury. You have heard all the evidence. After the incident in high school, I swore I'd never have a dog, yet..."

I swung my arm out to indicate my dog, but just as I did, he snagged a piece of bacon from my plate. "Objection!"

Bobby Jo's brow furrowed. "You're objecting to your own argument?"

"No," I said to her. Then I turned to my little thief. "I'm objecting to his behavior. Get down from there."

He scrambled to the ground.

"Now..." I inhaled deeply. "It is clear, then, that you enchanted me." I got serious. "You put me under your spell." I took her hand, trying to calm myself and settle everyone at the same time. "I love you, Bobby Jo. In fact, you've taught me what it means to love, *truly* love someone." I got on one knee.

Zoe gasped, and I heard Zack's "Whoa." But that was in the background because my heart was beating so loudly it almost drowned them out. Bobby Jo looked stunned. I hoped that wasn't a bad thing.

"So, I'm on one knee, *appealing* to you, pleading my case, if you will. You've made me a better person, counselor, and I want to continue to grow with you. To become a new and improved Nick each day and strive to become worthy of loving you." Objection came over and put his paws on my knee. "Good timing, boy," I commented. I snapped open the leather pouch strapped to his collar and withdrew a diamond ring. It was an heirloom I had secretly picked up when we went home and I introduced Bobby Jo to my mom. "Be careful how you respond, because I'm talking a life sentence here. Will you marry me?"

Zoe sniffled loudly.

Bobby Jo cupped my face, absolutely glowing. "Oh, Nick. I'd like nothing more than to be your wife."

I slipped the ring onto her finger, stood, and embraced her, kissing her as Zoe sobbed. Then when I went to thank them for helping me out, Zoe threw her arms around me.

"I'm so happy for you, Nick. You can be a big jerk sometimes, but you deserve this happiness that you've found."

I shook Zack's hand while the girls oohed and ahhed over the ring. "When I said a little distraction, I had no idea that you'd take it this far."

I socked him in the shoulder. I looked down and Harlan and Objection were sitting at my feet, wagging their tails. "This was the distraction. The proposal was... Well, it was probably the best decision I've ever made in my life."

A few months later, Zack and Zoe stood up for us. As would be expected, Bobby Jo made an absolutely gorgeous bride. My heart was more full of love than it had ever been. I felt like I'd finally gotten something right in my life, and it was 'case closed'.

NOTE FROM THE AUTHOR

Thank you for reading DEVIL'S ADVOCATE, part of my DEVILISH DESIRES SERIES. I hope you enjoyed it. Now that you've read the book, won't you please consider writing a review? Reviews are one of the best ways readers discover great new books. They don't need to be fancy or long, just a sentence or two honestly describing your opinion of/experience with the book. I would sincerely appreciate it.

Want more from M.J. Schiller?
Page forward for an excerpt from ~
FOUR AND TWENTY BLACKBIRDS
Fairytale Romance Series, Book One

FOUR AND TWENTY BLACKBIRDS

CHAPTER ONE

The birds began to sing. Or rather, shriek. The high-pitched noise was followed by the loud whir of wings as they lifted into the air. Isadore crooked her neck and watched them rise into the sky, obliterating the sun for a second, then she was forced to shade her eyes from its glare. Subtly, another noise replaced the first, coming from the same direction as the birds had and getting louder and louder with each passing moment.

What is...horses!

A chill washed over her that had nothing to do with the frigid water she was standing in. She had come with a dozen others to wash clothing in this stream. The water wasn't as deep as their normal creek bed, but it was closer to home, which was why they had chosen it. Nearby villages had been raided lately, and parents wanted their daughters nearby. She scanned the horizon and saw it. The wisp of smoke that meant others had been to their village.

Her warning burst from her mouth at the same time the mounts erupted from the tree line surrounding the watering hole.

"Riders!"

She moved as quickly as she could in the waist-deep water, releasing the shift she had been washing, letting it slowly drift away as the quiet idyllic scene of moments before changed into a nightmare. Horses came charging into the water from the banks, and women screamed as they attempted to flee but were caught up in the hands of riders. She searched for her sister, Ysmay, and caught sight of her red dress. A man had his arm around her neck and shoulders as he dragged her from the water, kicking and screaming.

"No! Ysmay!" She began to wade in that direction, frustrated by the resistance of the water and the weight of her dress. All she could do was cry out and watch as the man hauled her sister onto his mount and plopped her in front of him. He laughed and pulled on his horse's reins, twisting its head back to the bank. "No. Let her go." Ysmay at sixteen was two years her senior, but, as she was smaller framed, people often mistook them for twins.

Ysmay turned. Isadore couldn't hear her but read her lips. "Run, Izzy!"

Her view of Ysmay was cut off when a soldier and his steed cut between them, a yard away. The man grabbed a younger girl, who couldn't have been more than ten, and she shrieked. With dismay, Izzy realized that it was too late to help Ysmay, but maybe she could at least save this one girl. Isadore struggled forward and lunged at the last second to latch onto the girl's leg before she could be plucked from the stream. Getting her feet under her, Isadore reached up further to try to claw the girl from the man's grasp and almost succeeded. But she was so focused on prying his fingers from the girl's arm that she didn't see the sword in his other hand until it was too late.

She managed to whirl so that the broadside of the sword didn't connect with her face, but the solid blow to the temple area knocked her several feet. The fury of noise about her was drowned out as she sank under the surface of the water. Everything was muffled, save for the ringing in her ear, but she was unable to determine if that was a sound or simply a sensation. Her head was heavy, and she would have slipped into unconsciousness and drowned had she not, in her flailing, cut her foot on a rock. The sharp pain kept the blackness at bay. She blinked, looking up as a splotch of crimson floated eerily by. Something knocked against her, and she spun to find herself face to face with a corpse. Mistress Blackeney drifted past, her eyes wide but unseeing, her throat slashed, and a steady stream of blood coloring the water surrounding them. The mistress was her best friend Thea's grandmother and was more of a grandmother to Isadore than her own. In her horror, Isadore scrambled upright again, breaking the water and sputtering, disconcerted by the return of the noise and action all around her, and the fact that the girl she'd been trying to save, and the rider who had been attempting to steal her, were nowhere in sight. Had she lost her senses after all?

She didn't have much time to consider it as a new agony assaulted her when her single braid was yanked, dragging her against a boot and stirrup. As the rider bent over his horse, his voice was near, although she couldn't see him with her head forced down by his grip on her hair. She could, however, see the sword he threatened her with.

"Get on this horse or I'll run you through."

The blade was at eye level, giving her an idea. She took a breath and dove under the water. The sudden motion threatened to drag her captor from his saddle, so, like she'd hoped, he reflexively brought his sword hand in to brace himself against the side of the horse. The blade sliced her hair freeing her and leaving him holding her limp braid.

If she tried to swim away from the ruckus, he would no doubt catch her. Her only choice was to make her way once more into the middle of the fray.

When she surfaced for air, she was in much shallower water and able to move more quickly than before. She heard the man with her braid cursing behind her and striving to rotate his horse.

"Get her!" he screamed, but everyone else was involved in their own skirmish, and she was able to make it ashore.

Some of the raiders had hung back, out of the water, but the nearest was several yards off. Hearing the shouts, though, he twisted in his saddle and spotted her. He tugged on the reins and spurred his horse to pursue her. Trying to pull her wet skirts up to free her feet, Isadore ran as fast as she could, knowing he would be on her in seconds, and that all hope would be lost. But luck was with her, and the horse slid on the muddy bank giving her precious time to escape.

Looking over her shoulder, she saw her neighbor, Avalon, who had also managed to make her way to shore, captured by the man who had been chasing her and another from the group on shore. Izzy's gaze connected with Avalon's, and a stab of despair cut through her. She turned away and kept running.

TO READ WHAT HAPPENS NEXT, PURCHASE FOUR AND TWENTY BLACKBIRDS.

ALSO FROM M.J. SCHILLER

ROMANTIC REALMS COLLECTION:

TAKEN BY STORM
AN UNCOMMON LOVE
LEAP INTO THE KNIGHT
LADY OF THE KNIGHT
A KNIGHT TO REMEMBER

ROCKING ROMANCE COLLECTION:

TRAPPED UNDER ICE
ABANDON ALL HOPE
BETWEEN ROCK AND A HARD PLACE
ROCK ME, GENTLY
MIDNIGHT MELODY

LOVE AND CHAOS SERIES:

ROCKED BY GRACE
ROCKED BY LOVE
ROCK IT TO THE MOON
ROCK OF SALVATION

REAL ROMANCE COLLECTION:

UPON A MIDNIGHT CLEAR
THE HEART TEACHES BEST
DAMAGE DONE
BLACKOUT
HOMETOWN HEARTACHE
TAKE A CHANCE ON ME

DEVILISH DESIRES SERIES:

TO HELL IN A COACH BAG
DAMNED IF I DO
THE DEVIL YOU KNOW
SATAN, LINE ONE
PITCHFORK IN THE ROAD
SIN WORTH THE PENANCE
HELL HATH NO FURY
TEN MINUTES IN THE SIN BIN
DEVIL'S IN THE DETAILS
DEVIL'S ADVOCATE
HADE'S NIGHT (*Coming soon!*)

INSATIABLE FIRE SERIES:

BEATING IN TIME
LEAD ME ON
ROCK WITH THE RHYTHM
BASSIST'S INSTINCTS

HEARTS ON THE TABLE SERIES:

HEARTS FLUSH

FAIRYTALE ROMANCE SERIES:

FOUR AND TWENTY BLACKBIRDS (*Coming soon!*)
POCKETFUL OF RYE (*Coming soon!*)
SING A SONG OF SIXPENCE (*Coming soon!*)

ABOUT THE AUTHOR

Bestselling author M.J. Schiller is a retired lunch lady/romance-romantic suspense writer. She enjoys writing novels whose characters include rock stars, desert princes, teachers, futuristic Knights, construction workers, cops, and a wide variety of others. In her mind everybody has a romance. She is the mother of a twenty-seven-year-old and three twenty-five-year-olds. That's right, triplets! So having taught four children to drive, she likes to escape from life on occasion by pretending to be a rock star at karaoke. However, you won't be seeing her name on any record labels soon.

www.ingramcontent.com/pod-product-compliance
Lightning Source LLC
LaVergne TN
LVHW020043110826
845155LV00029B/626

* 9 7 8 1 9 3 9 2 7 4 8 9 2 *